PE
the
mo

listen, had to observe our every touch, only pushed us along.

I could *hear* her breathing, could feel her growing heat, and knew we were awakening something inside her. An intrigue that neither of us would fulfill unless she really begged.

She hadn't earned it.

Had tried to fucking end me.

And it was on that note that I came in my pants, Zian never having touched my bare skin, his grip knowing and steady.

I yanked on him in kind, infuriated that he soiled me in such a way but turned on at the same time, my pleasure humming up and down my spine. Totally unfulfilled yet oddly complete.

My gaze found our little voyeur as I kissed Zian through his own climax, his seed warming my torso. I invited her to join us with my eyes, to lick the sticky substance from my skin, but she remained in her little corner, those black irises pulsating with bemused innocence. Better for her because she was nowhere near ready to play.

Just as we would likely never allow it.

Intimacy required trust.

And she hadn't earned ours.

If anything, she'd only acquired our hate. Which was truly too bad because, in this place, she'd need an ally. And I wasn't all that inclined to help her after our last experience together. Although, I knew I would, purely out of obligation to her rare existence.

"I hope you can fly better than you did yesterday," I told her softly. "Because you're going to need those wings, little dove."

Zian sighed in contentment, his head hitting the pillow. "I give her a week, tops."

"Yeah?" I smiled, amused. "I give her maybe a day."

"Wanna make it a bet?"

"Absolutely."

"Cool. Winner gets on his knees," Zian decided.

Of course he would choose that. Because I would, too. "Works for me."

Noir Reformatory

The Beginning

NOIR REFORMATORY

THE BEGINNING

USA TODAY BESTSELLING AUTHORS

LEXI C. FOSS & J.R. THORN

WRITING AS
JENNIFER THORN

Noir Reformatory: The Beginning

Editing by: Outthink Editing, LLC

Cover Design: Christian Bentulan with Covers by Christian

Cover Photography: CJC Photography

Models: Danny Cevette, Skyler Simpson, & Jered Youngblood

Published by: Ninja Newt Publishing, LLC

Print Edition

ISBN: 978-1-950694-53-2

To Bethany, for squeezing us in on such short notice and for being an editing goddess. You're amazing and we heart you! <3

NOIR REFORMATORY

THE BEGINNING

Noir Reformatory
The Beginning

Happy birthday, Raven. Welcome to Noir Reformatory.

Not what every girl wants to hear on her eighteenth birthday, but I accepted my fate long ago. I was born with black wings, earning me a permanent jail sentence from day one.

A Noir angel for life.
That's fine.
I'll own this prison just like I did back home.
Even if it's ruled by two hot kings.

This reformatory isn't all-girls; it's co-ed. Which means I'm outnumbered ten to one by brutes with more brawn than brain. Not a problem. I thrive on aggression, and this place is riddled with it. A nightmare wrapped up in an ebony cloak.

Well, bring it on, boys.
Just try and claim me.

Note: This standalone MMF romance novel is part of the Paranormal Prison collection and the start of a brand-new MMF series by *USA Today* Bestselling Authors Lexi C. Foss & J.R. Thorn writing as Jennifer Thorn.

CHAPTER ONE

RAVEN

I ALWAYS CELEBRATED MY BIRTHDAY the same way: curled up with a ratty blanket under a silver moon. I'd find a place to hole up where I could stay out of harm's way just long enough to dream about what it would feel like to finally be free. A simple gift to myself, but easier said than done when growing up in juvie.

But today? Today I turned eighteen.

And it was time to stop dreaming.

A swift kick to my ribs sent me buckling over with a soundless gasp. I knew better than to cry out. My captors were thoroughly enjoying tonight's relocation.

"Thirteen inmates on today's flight," said a male. I couldn't see him, thanks to my blindfold, but I knew he would have sickeningly sweet blue eyes that veiled the cruelty the Nora liked to call justice.

As if to demonstrate, he knelt and lowered his voice as he whispered, "And we also have one raven." He ran his fingers through my hair, gripping the roots before yanking my head back. "Let's see if we can make her squawk."

No, the bastard didn't know my real name; he just had a lucky guess.

Raven.

The word described me well. I stood out with my jet-black hair and midnight wings that contrasted against my pale skin, noticeable even for a Noir angel. And if this douche wasn't careful, I'd peck one of his eyes out with the dagger I'd smuggled in my feathers.

"We have orders not to damage the goods," said another of my captors, sounding bored as the unmistakable ruffle of wings whispered over the low hum of the airship's engines.

It bugged me that the Nora thought they were so much better than me when, really, they deserved to be locked up much more than I did. What was my crime? Being born with black wings instead of white? Yeah, sorry. My bad.

My wings itched and strained against the buckled leather straps that pressed them uncomfortably into my back and dug my weapon's hilt into my spine. It was beyond insulting to be shoved into a contraption that flew through the air when I was perfectly capable of flight myself.

"Do you know where you're going? Noir Reformatory."

He said that like it was a threat, but I'd never heard of the place.

"I'm not sure a little thing like you will survive." He ran a finger down my throat and toward my breasts. "If you're a good pet raven, maybe I'll put in a good word with the Warden."

Yeah, I'd heard that before.

"Fuck off," I snapped, the comment earning me swift punishment. The guard shoved my face into the floor panel, sending pain exploding behind my eyes.

He jerked me up again by my arm. "And here I was trying to be helpful. Now I'm going to have to break something."

I licked away the blood from my busted lip and smiled.

The Nora hated it when I smiled.

"You're damaging the goods," the observer drawled, his tone turning exasperated.

"She's going to die anyway," said my captor as he squeezed my arm hard enough to leave a bruise. "I haven't seen a female in centuries, much less felt one underneath me. Why not have some fun? I won't say anything if you don't."

Silence indicated that the other guard was considering it.

But why hadn't he seen a female in centuries? What kind of place was Noir Reformatory?

The Nora dug his fingers into my hip, flipping me to face him before he slammed me against the wall. Something stiff pressed into my abdomen, and queasiness washed over me.

Growing up in an all-female-inmate juvenile center had left some things about the male anatomy to the imagination, but I'd had my share of run-ins with sex-starved guards to know what was about to happen. Breeding with prisoners was strictly forbidden, but that hadn't stopped the male guards from indulging their needs with some of the female instructors. They'd even touched a few of the older girls. And if these guards really thought I was about to die—

He leaned closer and drew in a long breath, taking in my scent as his fingers found the knot to my blindfold. "I want to see your fear," he whispered.

Fuck, this guy was sick.

The cloth fell, leaving me face-to-face with a Nora angel. His white wings spanned behind him and golden hair framed a stupidly gorgeous face, but his eyes were glassy and dead just like those of every other Nora I'd come across.

His hand slipped around my waist and I arched into him, letting him think I'd decided to be compliant. He smirked. "Well, look at that. The raven has learned to obey."

I shifted slightly, the angle giving my wings purchase against the wall behind me as my fingers caught the edge of my dagger. The Nora had been dumb enough to press me up against the release hatch.

Almost.

There.

Click.

Frigid air burst into the compartment as the door behind me flung into the sky. I'd gotten a good enough hold on my weapon to cut through one of the leather straps, and my left wing burst free as I plummeted, my captor having been thrown from me in the free fall.

The moment of elation mixed with raw terror when the open appendage sent me into a frantic spiral. I clutched my wing back to my shoulders and focused on working my other wing free, but the cold air made my fingers go numb and I couldn't feel what I was doing.

Shouts rang out and I knew the Nora were after me, but this was the closest I'd ever gotten to freedom in my life. Fuck if they were going to catch me now.

Willing all my focus and strength into the task as my body plunged in a chaotic free fall, I hooked the dagger into the other strap and twisted. The snap sent the weapon tumbling from my hand, but at least I'd managed to free myself.

With both wings unencumbered, I resisted the urge to extend them out. I'd learned that an uncontrolled free fall would only be made worse if I panicked. That was a good way to break my wings.

It was impossible to know how close I was to hitting the ground, but given the temperature after escaping the airship, I should definitely have enough time to correct my flight.

Probably.

Maybe.

It took all of my willpower to focus and let my instincts tell me which way was up and which way was down. I flicked my wings in short bursts, correcting my fall to keep myself from twisting until I was able to spread out my arms to slow my descent enough to reduce the damage I was about to take. Carefully, I snapped out my wings and grunted as my body shot upward from the sudden drag. When I managed to blink away the tears caused by the stinging winds and the raw ache running down my back, I drew in a sharp breath at my surroundings.

Nothing.

There was only darkness beneath me in all directions except for one lonely glow in the distance. This didn't feel like a place where the Nora would keep a women's penitentiary. At least at juvie, the prison had been surrounded by forest greenery. Here, though, there was no place to hide.

No place to land.

I realized that our destination was on an island, and I caught a warm air current that ran above choppy waters. I shot a glance over my shoulder, only to see that the darkness went on for as far as I could see.

What a bunch of bullshit.

The one time I got a chance at freedom, I had to be in the middle of fucking nowhere.

In my effort to gain a sense of my surroundings, I'd forgotten to keep tabs on my captors. A body slammed into me, and fingers wrapped around my wrist.

"Keep going," said a low voice. "You're going to need your strength. Don't waste your energy hovering." He smirked when I challenged his dark gaze.

I caught my breath when I discovered it was a Noir who had found me and not one of the guards.

A male Noir.

Then I realized he was still touching me.

I snatched my arm away and bared my teeth with a snarl. "Did you hit your head on the way down? We're free and you want to go *toward* the prison?"

He narrowed his eyes as long, wild, white-washed hair danced around his face, then he adjusted his flight to glide on my backdraft. "Suit yourself," he said, his words nearly escaping me on the breeze.

I considered the darkness again, looking back toward the horizon. I'd been on the airship for at least a few hours, and while I trained my wings as much as possible in a grounded juvie center, I couldn't go longer than an hour's flight, especially not without more sustenance than the fat lot of nothing they'd given me on the transport. The exertion of my escape already made me nauseatingly hungry, and my wings threatened to buckle from the jolt they'd received by breaking my fall.

I turned back toward the glow in the distance, where the dark-winged Noir inmates reluctantly approached followed by an airship overhead that monitored us.

"Damn it," I cursed, hating that the male Noir had been right.

Happy birthday, Raven.

Welcome to Noir Reformatory.

CHAPTER TWO

RAVEN

"WELL, DOESN'T THIS LOOK INVITING?" I murmured to myself as the glory of Noir Reformatory came into view.

Jagged spikes embellished every possible landing crevice along the walls and spires of the prison. Flitting shadows caught my eye as creatures prowled the coastline, leaving only one possible place to set down.

And it looked like a trap.

I waited for the other inmates to land first. Our group of fourteen added a small dash of black wings to the existing mass of angels grounded in the only open space available. A dusty field faced an empty stage, and the angels shuffled as they waited for the Warden to greet the new arrivals. I glanced upward, expecting the Nora to come and find me and punish me for my insolence, but only black-winged men fell from the sky.

Not encouraging.

I landed as far from the platform as I could, not wishing to draw attention to myself—although, with my injured wing, my landing was less than graceful.

I stumbled on impact, finding myself caught once again by the insufferable Noir whom I'd run into earlier.

"I told you not to waste your energy hovering," he chided, which earned a scowl from me.

"And I told you not to touch me."

He let me go and showed both palms in a display of surrender, for the first time giving me a glimpse of navy blue tattoos that wound up his arms in an intricate design, although it ended in a jagged line on his right bicep as if incomplete. "To be fair, this is the first time you've told me that."

I glowered. "Well, I was thinking it."

He smirked. "If I could read female minds, I wouldn't be here in the first place."

Were all men this annoying?

Ignoring the Noir, even if he was ruggedly gorgeous, I took stock of my surroundings. I could gawk at the hot, annoying Noir later.

By the looks of the sea of broad chests and massive wings much larger than my own, I was the only female here.

Odd.

Maybe my relocation had been a mistake. Once the Warden figured that out, I would be retrieved, right?

I mentally slapped myself. Since when were the Nora ever reasonable? No, I was going to have to figure this one out on my own.

My nostrils flared, taking in the variety of masculine scents around me.

The Nora had a burnt smell to them, like they'd been out in the sun for far too long. These Noir smelled different. Their cologne was murkier and not necessarily unpleasant. I frowned. Something about their aromas felt right. Too right. Like a mental mind trick of some kind.

Run, my instincts whispered. But there was nowhere to run to and no place to hide.

The other inmates preoccupied themselves by

measuring each other up rather than thinking about our surroundings or taking notice of my presence as the sole female in the yard. They probably didn't see me as a threat.

Dumbasses.

Dawn offered just enough light to show us that the stage at the center was still empty. The inmates grew increasingly restless, shuffling among one another while some cast wary glances at the airship still hovering above us. Groups segregated, already forming alliances that would keep them alive when fights would inevitably break out.

I should be making alliances, too. That was how I'd stayed alive in juvie.

"Something's not right," I whispered, not realizing that I was thinking out loud.

"Hmm," the Noir male agreed.

I glared at him, then I took a whiff. The scent caused me to narrow my eyes. "Why do you smell different?" He didn't have that wet-feather smell to him like some of the other Noir. He reminded me more of the ocean with salty breezes and an endless horizon that reflected in the deep blue of his eyes.

Breathtaking.

He smirked, no doubt taking note of my interest. "Is that your idea of a pickup line? Because it could use some work."

Tearing my gaze away, I forced myself to step back. I'd involuntarily wandered closer to him like a moth drawn to a flame.

I didn't like it.

"In your dreams," I quipped as a reflection of light caught my eye. I crouched as I focused on the object in the distance poking out from the sands. *Is that a sword?*

Dread washed over me as I turned my gaze to my feet. Messy streaks of the tiny pebbles covered another layer of grime underneath. I knelt, raking my fingernails through the sand to confirm my suspicions.

Dried blood.

The metallic scent of it was faint, but it was there. I had almost missed it with the plethora of male Noir screwing up my senses.

My eyes flashed to meet the tattooed Noir's gaze, and understanding passed between us.

This wasn't a welcome center.

This was a battle arena.

The first scream that ripped through the air sent chills down my spine. Instead of turning toward the disruption, I scanned the ground again, and this time I knew what I was looking for.

"Gotcha," I whispered as I scurried over to a buried dagger. I ripped the blade free from the sands and turned to find a smug Nora up on the stage. He spread his white wings and fluttered them so each glorious feather caught the light.

"Welcome to Noir Reformatory!" he bellowed as he waved his arms open wide in greeting. He smiled down with wicked cruelty at one of the Noir who sputtered up blood. The inmate clutched at a fresh wound that ripped a fist-sized hole through his chest. "Your orientation is simple," the Nora continued as his victim collapsed to the ground. "One-third of you must die."

He patted the machine gun that had erupted from the stage's floor on a mechanical arm. I'd only seen weapons like that at my juvie's perimeter. It took down anything that flew too close and encouraged all of the inmates to think twice before considering an escape, aerial or otherwise.

The Nora closed one eye as he aimed his finger at the crowd. The gun followed his movements. "Either I can pick volunteers or you can choose amongst yourselves." He smirked, his dark eyes opening wide and glinting with sick pleasure. "What'll it be?"

The angels glanced at one another. If they were anything like me, they'd been locked up all their lives with heartless, selfish creatures and this would be a simple decision to make.

Survival of the fittest.

Trust no one.

One of the Noir discovered a morning star buried in the sands and ripped it free, flinging it toward his nearest neighbor and connecting with his head. Gore splattered across the sands, and silence hushed over the inmates.

The Nora threw his head back as he roared with laughter. "Let the games begin!"

Chaos erupted.

I crouched and hugged my wings to my back as a handful of Noir launched into the air. I knew better than to test my strength against this group of inmates in the sky. My advantage would be on the ground, where my smaller wings wouldn't be as cumbersome as the males'.

The tattooed Noir inched closer to me and I stiffened, readying my blade to gouge a line down his beautiful throat. "Stick close to me," he growled under his breath.

Was this guy serious?

"Just stay out of my fucking way," I barked and moved to get past him, but he threw an arm out and sent me landing hard on the ground. Pain ricocheted up my spine as I bit down sharply on my lip. I wouldn't give the bastard the satisfaction of hearing me cry.

A javelin flashed through the air where I'd just been standing, and I blinked slowly.

"Are you a moron?" I snapped, although a shiver ran over my wings, the close call shaking me to my core. "Worry about yourself."

The Noir ignored my protests as he kicked up the javelin and readied it against a group heading our way, taking out one of the Noir with a perfectly aimed throw.

Shit.

Well, guess I had my alliance of two, whether I wanted it or not.

My ally dug out a pike from the sands and jabbed his weapon, keeping the group at bay and sending two of them launching into the air as they struggled to approach us.

While my Noir jabbed upward, I readied my dagger for two more who were closing in on the ground.

They grinned at me.

"Oh, look, the little female has a toy."

His buddy with a perfect smile winked. "You could poke an eye out with that thing." He adjusted his package.

"Although, it turns me on to see you handle a blade. Maybe we'll spare you and let you play with a real weapon after the Warden has his fun." He eyed the rest of his group and hefted his sword. "Only one-third of us have to die."

Rage snapped through me like the spark of a forest fire. I should have let him take out one of his buddies for me, but my dagger flew from my hand as instinct took over.

No one fucking disrespected me.

My weapon sailed through the air and pierced its target, eliciting a roar of pain as the Noir clutched at his eye.

"Oh, will you look at that. You were right," I said with a smirk, playing on his welcoming taunt about poking out an eye.

The tattooed Noir grunted as he thrust his weapon, piercing one of the Noir who flew overhead. The body landed next to us with a heavy thud. He regarded me with a deadly smile that had me holding my breath.

Before my ally could change his mind about protecting me—not that I needed much protecting—I ran over to my taunter writhing on the ground. I ripped the dagger from his eye and cut a clean line across his throat.

Killing came naturally to me, but it always took a little piece of my soul. A deep, cold sting radiated through my chest as I watched the light fade from the Noir's eyes. His buddies sneered at me, but their flaring nostrils said they'd rather fuck me than kill me. One tossed a fist at another's head, resulting in a brawl that had me backing away.

Let the morons kill themselves.

I could feel the tattooed angel watching me, and my wings twitched as I considered facing him. He'd saved my life, but I would be an idiot if I expected him to be any different from the rest of the inmates.

As far as I could see, I was the only female here, which meant I would be a trophy to fight over. If he thought he could charm me into compliance, then he had another think coming.

Before I could decide how to handle my ally, a cut-off scream caught my attention. I turned just in time to see a head separate from a Noir's body with a sickening pop, the remaining stump glinting with white bone and spurting a ridiculous amount of blood onto the sands. The sight made that deep, cold feeling spread all the way to my fingertips.

A shadow flitted away from the brutal attack, moving with deadly precision to the next set of inmates. Some tried to launch into the air, but they were too slow.

They didn't stand a fucking chance.

The shadow yanked down on their ankles and brought bodies crashing to the ground.

Heads flew as the Noir realized there was something terrifyingly powerful picking us off. They banded together, raising what weapons they'd procured from the bloody sands to fend off the new enemy.

The shadow blurred toward the largest grouping, slipping past their blows with ease as broad, black wings flashed, allowing me to catch a visage of the attacker.

To my surprise, it was a Noir. Dark hair framed pale blue eyes that calculated his next move with deadly speed as he lopped off another poor angel's head.

A lump caught in my throat when I realized he didn't have a blade. Didn't have any sort of weapon. He was beheading his victims with his bare hands.

"Fuck," my tattooed companion spat as he straightened, fixated on the show. He glanced up at the stage, where the Nora frantically shouted into a device. My ally swiped his face. "Novak's going to get us all killed."

He knew this psycho?

Clutching my bloodied dagger tightly, I stared at the back of his head while he was distracted by Novak's rampage. I probably shouldn't have acted on my next impulse, but the opportunity was just too good to ignore so I moved in.

Survival of the fittest.

Trust no one.

I was fast, but not fast enough. The tattooed Noir turned just in time for my dagger to miss its mark as his eyes sparked with surprise. My blade would have threaded between his beautiful feathers and hit his heart had he stayed still just a moment longer. Instead, my dagger sank into his rib cage, forcing him to release a grunt as he flared his wings to launch away from me.

He coughed up blood and grabbed at the hilt embedded in his chest. He didn't curse at me, or even appear all that angry. Rather, hurt blended with admiration in his gaze, making me wonder how long he'd been imprisoned. Because that look was too soft for our world, too humane.

The dark shadow roared with fresh rage as the blur of carnage paused, his lethal focus landing on me.

I bit down hard on my lip, realizing I'd horribly miscalculated the situation. They weren't enemies.

They were friends.

"Shit," I muttered as the dark shadow named Novak raced toward me with renewed vengeance.

The Nora on the stage shouted a command and then disappeared behind a door. The instant he was gone, the ground shook and green gas shot from the sands.

Dead. I was so dead.

And I probably deserved it for turning on my only perceived ally. Not the brightest move, but a necessary one. I did what I needed to do to survive. Always.

Letting instinct finally take over, I launched into the sky as the growl of the psycho named Novak chased me. He jumped, but I spotted a glint of chains keeping his wings bound. He was grounded.

He hit the sands hard and sputtered as the gas overwhelmed him, taking him down for good as his eyes rolled into the back of his head.

I pumped my wings with frantic thrusts to get away from the maniac who had beheaded the majority of the surviving inmates in the arena. I didn't know if the arena's gas had killed him or temporarily knocked him unconscious, but I wasn't going to stick around to find out. As I gained height, my heart lifted with relief but turned cold when I took in the sea of gore and dull, dead eyes staring back at me.

Then I spotted the weapon on the stage.

It was aimed straight at me.

I clutched my wings to my back and plummeted,

worrying about how I'd survive Novak and the noxious gas later. I definitely wouldn't survive a fire bullet straight through my chest.

Pain shot up my legs as I landed hard and crumpled into a ball, breaking more than a few of my primary feathers, which sent radiating stings down my back.

The bluish-green fog rolled over me like a greedy creature devouring its prey.

I drew in a breath as my eyes watered.

And darkness took me under.

CHAPTER THREE

SORIN

CITRUS. My nose twitched. *Why am I smelling oranges?*

No. Better question. Why was the scent of oranges going straight to my dick?

I groaned, turning to my side and seeking relief from my right hand. What I wouldn't give for a warm mouth to sink balls-deep into right now. "Zian," I muttered, searching blindly for him without opening my eyes. "Where the fuck are you?"

"Down here," he replied, sounding far more awake than me.

"Down where?"

"Under you."

I frowned. "You're definitely not fucking under me." Or I'd be playing with him already. "Get in bed."

"Can't."

"Why the fuck not?" I demanded.

"We have company."

"Novak doesn't give a shit." He knew Zian and I enjoyed fucking around. Sometimes he even watched. The bastard was a voyeur like that. Fortunately, I favored a good bout of exhibitionism and so did Zian. Except for right now, apparently, when I had my shaft throbbing in my palm. I gave it a good stroke, losing myself to the sweet

16

aroma assaulting my senses.

Until reason started to override my need.

Why am I losing my shit over sweet citrus, and where is it coming from?

"It's not Novak," Zian said softly, a note of wonder in his tone. "Definitely not Novak."

"What?" He wasn't making any sense. What the hell happened last night? Rolling onto my back, dick still in my hand, I squinted open an eye, expecting to see a hot sun bearing down on me.

And instead found a solid ceiling.

"The fuck?" I started to sit up, but reason had me pausing midway. The concrete slab was maybe two feet above me, making it an obstacle my forehead would definitely collide with if I finished the motion.

Lying back down, I glanced right. Another white wall. To my left was a set of bunk beds—which I must be on the top of on my side of the room—and a standard jail cell door at the foot of it.

Huh.

Not the quarters I woke up in for the last hundred years or so.

A window overlooking the water decorated the final wall, giving a politely false ambience to the otherwise drab room. "Where the fuck are we?"

"Great question," Zian replied. "An even better one is, who the fuck is she?"

"Who the fuck is who?" I asked, rolling off the top bunk to land deftly on my feet beside him.

He gestured to the bunk across from us with his chin while I fixed my loose-fitting pants.

A head of raven hair caused me to freeze, my dream sequence suddenly becoming a reality in my mind. I grasped my ribs, felt the healing bruise left over from where that cunning little bitch had thrown a dagger at me.

I'd been so awestruck by the sight of a female that I'd stupidly tried to protect her like one would a rare jewel. "She tried to kill me," I snapped, stalking toward her as Zian jumped off the lower bed.

There were a good ten feet between the bunks, giving him time to jump between us, his lean form solid muscle and incredibly lithe. He put his hands on my shoulders, holding me back. "We need her alive right now."

"Then I won't kill her," I replied. "I'll just return the favor of our acquaintance."

I tried to duck around him, but he moved with me in a timeless dance our bodies had formed throughout the decades together. It made him an excellent lover and sparring partner. Right now, I needed him to be neither. "Move, Z."

"Novak's gone," he cut in. "We need to find out what she knows before you go all crazed Noir male on her."

"Crazed Noir male?" I repeated, snorting. "I'm not going to rape her, Z. I'm just going to teach her a lesson she won't soon forget." One that involved working an apology from those full lips.

Her big black eyes popped into my mind, followed by her gorgeous face and elvin chin. She reminded me of a little fairy, her petite form dwarfed by my height and size. Only, she had fought dirty, her skills somewhat admirable for her age. Definitely untrained, nowhere near warrior status like me and Zian, but adequate for her survival.

"She threw a dagger at me," I said, irritated and turned on all over again.

"I know." Zian moved again, halting my progress forward and shoving me back with a palm against my bare chest. My wings hit the metal pole connecting the bunks, and I narrowed my gaze at him.

"Stop fucking around and let me wake her up."

"You can't kill her."

The word *yet* lingered between us.

Because we both knew Zian wasn't afraid of a little death.

"I said I wasn't going to, Z," I said, annoyed that he didn't seem to believe me. "I have better control than that."

"I know. I'm just…" He trailed off, huffing a breath and shaking his head. "I can feel Novak. He's not in pain, but he's not *here* either."

I frowned. "What do you mean?"

"He's cut himself off somehow. Or something has cut *him* off." Zian ran a palm over his face, his familial bond to Novak providing him with better insight into the situation than me. They were cousins, having known each other from birth. I was the friend they'd made later in life during our teen years while training to become Nora Warrior Angels.

Zian and I had hit it off right away. Novak took more work, his stoicism renowned. The male only spoke when he had something important to say, which was infrequent at best. He preferred to analyze and watch situations before acting on them.

Which told me he had cut through all those Noir yesterday for a reason. I just didn't know what it was because he'd done it without explanation.

And now, apparently, he was missing.

Awesome.

"If you don't trust me to wake her up, then you do it. Once she proves not to know anything, I want my turn." I folded my arms, proving I planned to keep my hands to myself until Zian gave me permission to play.

Zian ran his fingers through his midnight hair, the edges flopping back into his eyes as soon as he stopped. The dark strands rarely cooperated, preferring the just-out-of-bed look over any semblance of elegance. It matched his persona perfectly, his attitude rarely agreeing to assimilate to any given situation.

He was unforgivably Zian, never pretending to be anyone else.

And he certainly was not a good guy.

If I wanted to kill the dark-haired beauty, he wouldn't bat an eye. He just wanted to ensure she lived long enough to gather his details about Novak. Once she proved to know nothing—which I was certain would happen quickly—he'd hand her over with a flippant "Do your thing."

With a stiff nod, he turned toward the exquisite creature on the other bed. Her black wings were curled around her like a blanket, several of the feathers bent at angles that told me she'd injured herself in the arena.

My first instinct was to examine the breaks and help fix them.

Then I remembered the dagger she threw at me and cupped my side instead. Anger simmered inside me all over again, as well as a twinge of respect. She hadn't trusted me from the start, which marked her as intelligent. Because I would absolutely turn on her if required.

My life would always come first. As well as those of Novak and Zian.

We were brothers by trade, an unbreakable triad at our old prison, and we'd rule this one, too. Wherever the fuck we were. "What did that Nora call this place? Noir Reformatory?"

Zian snorted, his dark eyes on the female as he examined her svelte form. "Yeah. The guards on the flight here said it was a step up from our last accommodations. I think he lied."

"I think he lied, too," I drawled, taking in our cell once more. "But at least we have a view of the water."

"Assuming that's even real."

"True." The Nora adored fucking with our minds.

Well, not all Nora.

Just the guards in charge of this prison system.

Because the three of us used to be Nora before our wings turned black. And we weren't mind-fucking assholes in our past roles. We favored peace. Until a situation required us to choose loyalty to each other over that of the Nora.

Which led to our imprisonment a hundred years ago. They claimed all we needed to do was repent, and we did to no avail. Now we chose to survive.

"Why isn't she awake?" Zian demanded, kicking her bed.

"She's frail and young," I mused, taking in her petite frame once more. "I'd guess eighteen, maybe nineteen." Angels stopped outwardly aging around their twenty-fifth year, but our auras gave us away. "She's inexperienced."

"Very," Zian agreed, crouching by her bed. "But she

20

nailed you good with that blade."

"I'd call it luck. However, she nailed Reese in the eye before slitting his throat."

"Who trained her?"

"No idea, but she needs improvement." Her throwing arm impressed me. Her flight skills, not so much.

Zian arched a dark brow. "Aww, are you volunteering to help her out again? Because that didn't work very well for you last time."

"If she wants training, she'll have to earn it," I muttered, thinking about all the ways I'd enjoy making her pay for turning against me. She should have just accepted my generosity. I wouldn't have required anything in return. Now? Now I'd make her beg for so much as a hint of how to survive in this new hellhole.

In fact, I'd probably make her life hell just for fun.

She deserved it and worse for trying to fucking kill me.

Zian reached out to draw his finger down her exposed spine between her wings, the touch intimate and typically reserved for mates. That wasn't why he did it. He wanted to see if she truly slept, his senses picking up her breathing rhythm at the same time mine did.

She flew around—literally—and tangled herself in her broken wings, reminding me of a youngling trying to fly for the first time.

I snorted. "Not so skilled now, is she?"

"Nope," Zian drawled, having taken a step back to stand beside me in solidarity, his arms folding over his chest to mimic my stance. "What's your name?"

"Fuck you," she returned, her hair wild as she finally surfaced from her cocoon of unkempt feathers. She sputtered, blowing the strands from her face and going to crouch in her little bunk.

I arched a brow at her. "That's not a smart defense, sweetheart. You have nowhere to go but forward, which means I could have you pinned to that mattress in two seconds flat. And be inside that sweet cunt in less than five seconds after that."

She growled, and it was the most adorable sound I'd

ever heard. Even Zian seemed to be amused by it. Or maybe it was my threat. He knew I'd never follow through on it. I was a lot of things, but I valued consent. Just like he did. Made the victory so much hotter.

"Touch me and I'll bite you," she threatened.

"That's foreplay, baby," Zian replied. "Keep going."

This time she snarled like a wildcat caged and awaiting release. I smirked and shook out my hair, noting the dried blood fraying the white strands. There was a shower in the corner of the room that would fix the problem. I'd take advantage of it when we finished here.

"What happened to Novak?" I asked, taking Zian's line and wanting to get this interrogation over with.

"Novak?" she repeated, frowning. "How the hell would I know what happened to your psychotic friend?"

"Because I saw you take off in a flurry of wings when the gas hit. You were one of the last ones standing," Zian accused.

I hadn't known that, having been taken down quickly thanks to the damn wound in my rib cage. Now I understood why he was hell-bent on questioning her. "What did you see?"

Rather than reply, she glanced around the cell, her black eyes noting every detail in a matter of seconds.

Yep. Definitely intelligent.

But also very young. "What did you do to earn your black wings?" I wondered out loud, curious about what sin she could have committed at such an early age. Zian, Novak, and I had all been closer to six decades old before our Fall. This girl couldn't be any older than twenty, tops.

"None of your fucking business," she retorted, finally meeting my gaze again. "You may have helped me out in the arena, but that doesn't mean I owe you shit. So put your dick away. It's not happening."

Both my eyebrows shot up as I met Zian's equally startled gaze. "Are we speaking the same language, Z? Because I swear I didn't proposition her."

"You did mention her cunt. Maybe she took that as an offer rather than a threat?" he said conversationally.

22

"I suppose. I meant it subjectively to point out her inferior position."

"I know. She must not have understood. Perhaps we should speak more plainly?"

"Or you two jackasses could stop acting like I'm invisible," she suggested, her tone bitter. "I'm right fucking here."

"Oh, are you?" I bent down to peer into her eyes. "Sorry, I couldn't see you in your makeshift cave. Do you feel safe in there, sweetheart? Is that why you're hiding?"

Zian moved in that blindingly fast way of his, snatching her ankle and yanking her out onto the floor. She shrieked, shuffling backward on her hands to brace herself against the door.

I chuckled, shaking my head. "Still cornered, baby."

"Stop fucking around and tell us what you saw. Where's Novak?" Zian demanded.

She visibly shivered, the first ounce of fear permeating the air as she realized the gravity of her situation—trapped in a room with two virile males. We could overpower her in less than a second and take her repeatedly, and something told me no one would jump in to stop us. Because that was the kind of prison we'd landed in, one where inmates fought for survival.

And she'd been put into a cell with two of the toughest Noir in existence.

That was not an exaggeration but a fact. One she was going to learn quickly if she didn't start answering Zian's questions.

"I'm not going to fucking ask again," Zian seethed, stepping toward her.

Yet he'd worried about me overreacting. Typical.

I grabbed him by the neck, pulling him back when he advanced another step. "Give her a minute to think."

"There's nothing to fucking think about. She was aware when the gas started. What happened after that?"

"Some jackass Nora with a gun tried to shoot me down with fire bullets," she said, her eyes wild with fury. "So I crashed into the ground and suffocated on the gas with the rest of you. End of story. Happy?"

Zian eyed her for a long minute, then looked at me. "You believe her?"

"She tried to kill me," I reminded him. "I don't trust a damn thing about her."

He lifted a shoulder. "Fair enough. Go ahead and teach her a lesson. I could use some entertainment."

I nearly smiled, aware of his tactic. He knew fear would drive any additional details from her that might prove pertinent to our situation. "Gladly." I rolled my neck and took a menacing step forward.

She jumped to her feet in a lithe move, her palms flying upward in defense. "I'm sorry about the dagger, okay? I was just trying to survive the fight."

"Something I had been trying to help ensure happened," I pointed out, advancing on her.

Her fist came toward my jaw, and I caught it with ease, then snatched her opposite hand before she could think to use it. Pinning both wrists above her head beneath one palm, I used my opposite one to encircle her throat.

"Not smart, little girl," I whispered, moving into her personal space to slide one thigh between her legs. "Tell me your name."

"Why?" Strength radiated from her tone even while terror dilated her pupils. An intoxicating combination that had my dick hardening again in intrigue.

Or maybe it was the fact that I hadn't touched a female in over a hundred years.

I wouldn't act on it.

But I would fantasize about it later, maybe with Zian. We used to share women all the time, a distant memory I longed to repeat.

"Perhaps I want to know what name to use when issuing you commands in bed later," I whispered against her ear, smiling as a trail of goose bumps pebbled down her exposed arms.

She wore one of those sleeveless halter shirts that tied at the back of the nape and draped over the front, allowing her wings freedom while covering all the sexy bits. No bra, just a thin layer of fabric concealing her hardening nipples. I couldn't tell if that was a result of fear or arousal, or perhaps a mixture of both.

I met her dark gaze and noted the hint of defeat lurking in her black depths. "Mmm, yes, you're learning," I praised, releasing her and stepping back. "And here I wasn't planning on teaching you a damn thing."

Turning around, I went to sit on Zian's bed, ignoring the broken dove by the door. She clearly knew nothing.

"I need you to add seven new marks," I told Zian, referring to my tats.

"With what?" he asked, glancing around. "I don't have any of my tools here."

"I guess we'll have to barter for them."

He lifted a shoulder. "Or I'll make some, but it'll take a bit to gather supplies."

"I'll wait, then. Might have additional ones for you to add by then."

He glanced at the female and scoffed out a "Likely." Not because I'd kill her, but because I'd probably end up killing others on account of her.

I didn't have to like her to feel a need to protect her.

It was ingrained in my warrior blood.

Females were rare, male angels outnumbering them ten to one in most cases. Hence the reason I hadn't seen a woman in almost a century.

Noir females were even more exceptional considering it required significant sins to acquire black wings. It made me wonder what she could have done to earn her dark feathers. Given how easily she'd turned on me with that blade, I supposed it wasn't too far-fetched to assume she'd done the same to someone else. Maybe even killed them.

Zian caught my gaze and cocked his head slightly, trying to tell me something.

I stretched, pretending to laze about, and followed the direction of his tilt to find the swiveling camera in the ceiling near the window. Not wanting to make it obvious I'd found the reformatory's little spying device, I went to lean against the wall just beside the glass, hands in the pockets of my jeans. I rolled my shoulders and neck around slowly, taking in the angles of the device and studying the technology.

"No sound," I said after a few sweeps of the area and the rest of the room.

"You sure?"

I nodded, my technical expertise rarely failing me. "Yeah, it's visual surveillance only. They probably want to see how long it takes us to destroy her." Why else put a ripe young female in a room with two former warrior males who hadn't experienced a woman's touch in forever?

Zian shook his head. "Sick fucks."

I agreed with a sharp nod, thinking about the Nora guards I'd come to hate. "Either we give them a show or we see how long it takes for them to give up and move the bait elsewhere."

Zian checked out said bait quivering against the wall, his lip curling in disgust. "I vote for the latter."

"Sounds good to me." I flopped down onto his new bed, hands tucked behind my head. "I still want a blow job, Z. Maybe our guest without a name will learn something from it."

"Doubtful." He joined me on the mattress, his expression dark. "There's no way she could handle either one of us, even with training."

Too true, I thought, glancing at her as Zian grabbed my throat. "Look away, little dove," I advised her. "The men are about to play, and we wouldn't want to harm your innocent sensibilities."

The girl's aura screamed *virgin,* her hard exterior protecting an obviously soft interior. I could see it in her eyes now as I threaded my fingers through Zian's thick hair and pulled his mouth to mine.

He bit down on my lower lip in reprimand, hating when I tried to control him. Mmm, I adored this constant fight for control between us.

I pushed; he shoved back.

I demanded; he countered with his own command.

It was why Novak enjoyed watching us—he never knew

who was going to win our little sensual battles.

"Where do you think he is?" I asked, my grip tightening in his hair to pull in the way I knew he both loved and hated.

Zian released my throat and palmed my cock, squeezing it roughly to punish me in kind. "He's alive and that's what matters," he replied, knowing I referred to Novak. There was no one else I could be talking about.

I growled as Zian gave me a firm stroke through the pants. "That's not what I want."

"I know." He yanked hard on my dick, drawing a hiss of pain from me. "You'll take what I give you."

"Bastard."

"Asshole," he countered.

A little gasp had me looking away from him and to the female in the corner again, her cheeks rosy red. "I warned you to look away, little dove."

Zian gave me another stroke, this one even harsher than the last. "Focus."

"Oh, I'm fucking focused." Both on him and the beautiful creature watching us play. It was as if she couldn't look away, her gorgeous lips parted on a gasp that resembled a slight pant of surprise. Her citrusy scent spiked, causing me to groan. "More." I meant it for Zian and for her, because I liked the way she smelled.

His mouth found mine once more, his kiss punishing and desperate. I realized immediately what he needed and why. His cousin had gone missing, and he craved a distraction, one that would help him refocus with refreshed senses.

So I gave it to him with my lips and tongue and hands, exploring his body in the way I knew he preferred and taking his shaft into my palm in a practiced manner. I thought of the little darling while we fooled around, considered what it would be like to force her to lick us clean after we finished, and found my orgasm mounting by the second.

Pent-up rage and aggression from the arena caught me in the balls, spurring on our movements. Knowing she had to watch, had to listen, had to observe our every touch, only pushed us along.

Because I could *hear* her breathing, could feel her growing heat, and knew we were awakening something inside her. An intrigue that neither of us would fulfill unless she really begged.

She hadn't earned it.

Had tried to fucking end me.

And it was on that note that I came in my pants, Zian never having touched my bare skin, his grip knowing and steady.

I yanked on him in kind, infuriated that he soiled me in such a way but turned on at the same time, my pleasure humming up and down my spine. Totally unfulfilled yet oddly complete.

My gaze found our little voyeur as I kissed Zian through his own climax, his seed warming my torso. I invited her to join us with my eyes, to lick the sticky substance from my skin, but she remained in her little corner, those black irises pulsating with bemused innocence. Better for her because she was nowhere near ready to play.

Just as we would likely never allow it.

Intimacy required trust.

And she hadn't earned ours.

If anything, she'd only acquired our hate. Which was truly too bad because, in this place, she'd need an ally. And I wasn't all that inclined to help her after our last experience together. Although, I knew I would, purely out of obligation to her rare existence.

"I hope you can fly better than you did yesterday," I told her softly. "Because you're going to need those wings, little dove."

Zian sighed in contentment, his head hitting the pillow. "I give her a week, tops."

"Yeah?" I smiled, amused. "I give her maybe a day."

"Wanna make it a bet?"

"Absolutely."

"Cool. Winner gets on his knees," Zian decided.

Of course he would choose that. Because I would, too. "Works for me."

CHAPTER FOUR

RAVEN

WHAT THE ACTUAL FUCK?

The two gorgeous angels slept, each on their own bunk, after finishing their version of "playing."

I sat in the corner with my wings around me like protective walls as I peered through the feathers at my new cellmates. I hated how the tattooed Noir had immediately caught on to the childish habit I reverted to when I felt truly caged. It hadn't happened in a long time, but I was trapped in an enclosed room with two psychos who smelled…

Delicious.

I closed my eyes and let out a hard breath through my nose, trying to get rid of their intoxicating scent. The salty breeze the tattooed Noir reminded me of had spiked into something new when he and the one he called "Z" had pleasured each other.

Like salt and melted caramel.

The two of them together resembled mesmerizing

magic that was impossible to ignore. Their battle of give-and-take had been honed to an art form that was difficult not to envy. I'd never had an ally like that, much less a lover of my own.

I'd never needed one, but then again, I'd never been to Noir Reformatory.

Watching them had done something to me I couldn't explain. Even now my skin tingled and my tongue flashed out onto my lips, almost able to taste the hint of sweetness that left hot and cold sensations zipping through my core.

My brain tried to overrule the waves of need cresting through my body to remind me that this was just a biological reaction to compatible mates. The scent was especially overpowering given that I had never experienced it before, and there were two compatible males who had just pleasured themselves mere feet away from me, leaving their arousal lingering in the air.

I'd clearly been placed in this cell quite deliberately. A female's reaction to a compatible mate could make her go crazy if not dealt with appropriately.

And, given my circumstances, I was about to take a trip to Loony Town.

When I opened my eyes again, the angels were still there tormenting me with their sated pleasure. Their scent bathed the room and weakened me with every breath I was forced to take.

I didn't dare move or unfurl from my protective cage, so I continued to watch.

The tattooed one slept on the lower bunk, his long white-blond hair still damp from his shower, and it layered over his naked body like folds of silk. His chest rose and fell with rhythmic movements that had me mesmerized. Watching him sleep was almost as fascinating as watching him with Z. He hadn't had any trouble with me observing him when he creamed his pants or when the other one exploded on his chest—and both had been insanely hot, although if asked, I would take that to my grave.

Likewise, he'd faced me during his shower, amused as I watched each droplet carve a line over perfectly shaped muscles. Z had been equally as entertained by my fascination, quietly studying me as he lazed on the top bunk without a word.

They horrified and enthralled me, and they both knew it.

In their defense, the tattooed one had told me to look away, but his eyes had beckoned me when Z touched him.

Perhaps he'd wanted me to join them, but I'd rather succumb to insanity than give these two psychos my virginity. In fact, I still didn't understand why they hadn't just overpowered me. They'd made it very clear how little control I had in this situation. If I affected them even a fraction of how they affected me, I was bewildered that they had been able to resist the temptation at all.

Given that we were compatible mates, I had a feeling I would have enjoyed it whether I wanted to or not.

Maybe that was why they hadn't. To punish me for my betrayal.

If so, it was working. The persistent ache between my legs only worsened with each inhale of the fog of salty caramel in the air that I couldn't escape.

A small sound left my throat, and I clamped a hand over my mouth, realizing I'd just whimpered.

Again, *what the actual fuck?*

I flashed a glare at the tattooed Noir, but he still slept, even if I might have imagined the small smirk at the edge of his mouth.

A blessed distraction came in the sound of a small chittering animal that pushed itself through a crevice in the wall.

A mouse.

It sniffed the air, its tiny whiskers flicking as it flinched left and right before spotting me. It froze, and its beady eyes watched me.

I loved animals of every kind, and I instantly lowered my wings with a soft, delicate motion so as not to frighten it. "Hello," I whispered, putting a layer of sweetness to my voice that animals seemed to respond favorably to. "What's your name, little guy?"

The mouse flicked his whiskers a few more times before deciding I wasn't a threat. He scurried to my knees and sniffed my fingers. His mind brushed mine, and I smiled. Not all animals could communicate with me, but those with a touch of magic could. Magic was like stray dust— sometimes it stuck to things it shouldn't.

He asked me to tell him my name first.

"Well, I'm Raven, if you must know."

He squeaked, telling me it was a fun name because I looked like a raven with all my silky feathers.

I ruffled my primaries with pride. As far as I knew, I had been born with my dark feathers and had done nothing to deserve my imprisonment, but no one would ever believe that. Animals, though, they didn't judge. That was what I loved about them.

"So, are you going to tell me your name now? I told you mine."

The mouse admitted that he didn't have a name but said I was welcome to give him one.

"Aww, you're so sweet," I murmured as I used my pinky to stroke his small head. He leaned into the gentle touch. "I think I'll call you Mousey Mouse. Do you like that?"

He squeaked with approval and then went still. His little heart pattered against our fragile connection as his reflexes kicked in.

I saw why a moment later when the tattooed angel shifted his weight and I caught him staring right at me. When his gaze flicked to the tiny animal on the ground, Mousey Mouse screeched and scurried back through the crack in the wall, taking my moment of peace with him.

"Mousey Mouse?" the Noir mused. "How unoriginal."

My own instincts kicked in, reflexively wrapping my wings around myself in a cocoon of protection. "You have a better name?"

He frowned. "I don't name my snacks."

"Snacks!" I shrieked. "You will not eat Mr. Mousey Mouse!"

He chuckled and sat up, flexing his wings before settling them to his back. "Or what, *Raven*?"

32

I glowered at him with raw hatred. It wasn't a big deal that he knew my name now, but I didn't like how it sounded on his tongue, so sultry and... seductive.

The scent of an ocean breeze kicked up a notch, making me pinch my nose, although that didn't really help. It was as if his scent wrapped around me and seeped into my pores until I would be driven mad by it.

The Noir chuckled again, clearly amused by my reaction.

"Will you two knock it off?" a sleepy voice chided from above. "A place like this won't give us downtime for long. We're going to need our rest."

The tattooed Noir lightly punched the upper bunk, making Z swat at him from above. "Relax, Drill Sergeant." He settled onto his back, fanning out his wings so as not to crush them with his heavier, male body. He threaded his hands behind his head and closed his eyes as I watched his every movement.

"Get some sleep, Raven," he said when I hadn't moved.

"I'm not tired," I lied. My eyelids were as heavy as boulders.

"It's in your best interest," he promised as one hand slipped downward to his growing bulge.

Again? I wondered, bewildered. *I can't handle more of this*—

"You're pouring your scent into the room, and it's making me want to go for round two," he replied as if hearing my thoughts, something I knew was impossible. "But Z's right. We don't know what's coming tomorrow and need to be physically prepared." He stretched and shamelessly adjusted himself. "If you can't control your glands, then sleep might turn it off before you get me too worked up."

Heat raged up my neck, and I was grateful he had his eyes closed.

"Oh," I murmured, royally embarrassed that he could smell me.

Scurrying back toward my own mattress, I made a nest out of my wings before resting my head down on my primaries. As a female, I didn't weigh much, which came in handy when fighting with speed—or when trying to sleep without touching whatever grimy sheets the prison had issued.

I shifted until there was a large enough peephole through my cocoon to peer at my cellmates. I'd make sure he fell asleep before I would dare close my eyes, but I wasn't sure if I should believe the small rise and fall of his chest.

I tried anyway.

Sleep seemed impossible. I watched the tattooed Noir for a long time, hoping I could relax enough to fall asleep, but all I could do was stare at him with my heart racing as if I were a mouse he was going to eat.

"You're still awake," he noted, making me flinch and confirming that he hadn't been sleeping at all. "The name's Sorin, little dove." He cracked one eye open and smiled at me.

"Why would you tell me your name?" I asked, not opening my protective cocoon.

His smile grew. "In case you want to scream it when I take you. Because if you don't close your eyes and go to sleep, that's what's going to happen."

"Fuck off," I snapped, earning another chuckle as I screwed my eyes shut.

Somehow, I eventually drifted off to the sound of Sorin's sultry amusement.

* * *

FRESH BATCHES OF INMATES had trickled in over the last few days, battered and bloodied from the arena, and the local cells slowly filled to the brim.

I had a bad feeling this was just the beginning.

Z confronted a few weakened prisoners for information. Sorin reminded me that everyone here had survived the arena, so I had better watch my back if I tried anything funny.

Especially because I was still the only female.

Z's findings didn't turn up anything on his friend Novak, but rumor had it that Noir Reformatory was a new prison meant to hold the worst of the worst, so I still wasn't sure what the hell I was doing here. Mistake or not, I needed to figure out how I was going to escape, and I needed to do it fast.

Until then, I had to survive, which meant playing my part as the claimed female.

Z, which I eventually learned was short for "Zian," kept watch while Sorin manhandled me through the breakfast line and to our seats in the corner, where we could put our backs against the wall. The duo had taken it upon themselves to hold me hostage as their little trophy until they decided what to do with me or determined if I could be useful to gather intel on their friend Novak. Zian seemed to believe me that I hadn't seen anything, but he was getting antsier by the day. If either of them decided I was no longer valuable, or at least mildly entertaining, I could kiss breathing goodbye.

I thought about making a run for it more than once, but by the hungry looks from the other inmates, I considered myself lucky that I wasn't mauled on a nightly basis. Not that Sorin and Z made it easy on me.

Oh, the routine itself wasn't bad.

Breakfast.

Time in the yard—no flying permitted, of course.

Dinner.

Back to our cells.

Unfortunately, the last bit was where I wanted to kill myself, which was likely the point.

The salty caramel mixture burst sweet flavor across my tongue the instant Zian and Sorin started sparring again. This was often how they began their nightly ritual of testosterone release, usually ending in a sensual display that had me panting with need.

Tonight wasn't any different.

The two angels fought just as beautifully as they fucked. Even in the small confines of the cell, they blurred, their midnight wings painting a smear of oil against a tapestry of white-washed walls. Sorin moved like a violent storm, his brilliant hair floating around him in an arc as he spun and moved.

Zian's fighting style was simple but effective. He absorbed each heavy blow as if immune to pain. He returned some of his own with calculated precision and far more speed than I would have credited the male, earning a grunt when he landed his fist into the soft underside ligament where Sorin's wing attached to his body—a sensitive spot for a Noir.

Sorin stumbled and barreled into me, making me squeak as I failed to dodge in time. "Watch it!" I snipped, pushing Sorin's weight to no avail.

The angel growled, and his nostrils flared as he shoved me into the center of the cell. "Stay out of my way," he warned. "Unless you want to stop hiding and learn how to fight." An evil grin flashed across his face as he took a step toward me, making me back up only to find Zian trapping me from the other side. "What do you say, Z? Should we teach the little dove how to take care of herself? I'm tired of playing protector while we decide what to do with her."

I had a feeling the two Noir were going just as stir-crazy as I was, trapped with each other's scent driving us mad. They'd pleasured one another night after night after a bout of intense sparring, but they both only seemed to become more frenzied, with each session longer and more violent than the last.

"I don't know," Zian mused as he wrapped my arms behind my back, pinching my wrists together. "Maybe we should just teach her how to take a punch instead."

Sorin growled as he towered over me, trapping me between him and Zian. I held my breath as I stared up into the raw violence raging in his eyes. "Maybe she should learn to take something a bit stronger than a punch."

I pulled my gaze away, the heady musk of arousal from the two of them made me dizzy, but I wasn't about to just roll over and play dead.

He grabbed my chin, angling my face up to look at him. When Sorin's finger got too close to my mouth, I bit down—hard.

He cursed and yanked back, but I didn't let go. My jaw

ached when he dragged me away from Zian and slammed me against the bars until I released my hold.

"Bitch," he cursed, nursing his bleeding hand.

I spat on the floor and was about to do something stupid—like try to attack Sorin, an experienced warrior—when the cell doors opened.

I dumbly stared at the free space until a voice echoed through a staticky intercom. "All inmates to the yard for mandatory flight training. Failure to comply will result in fatal gassing in all cell units."

Flight training?

"They're going to have us fly?" Zian mused out loud. "That can't be fucking good."

Sorin grunted in agreement before pushing past me, making me stumble. "Come on, little dove. Stay close to us."

"What if it's another arena run?" I asked, unable to hide the tremor in my voice.

He glanced over his shoulder, his gaze smoldering with unhidden need. "If anyone is killing you today, it's going to be me."

That's comforting.

The yard typically had a long, wired ceiling that kept us grounded, but today it was rolled back to expose the smoky sky that never seemed to allow us any sunlight. I craved to launch myself up into it and soar above the clouds. No matter how shitty the weather, the sun was always waiting just beyond the horizon.

My wings flexed outward, and I released a breath of relief after having had them scrunched up for so long. It would feel amazing to fly, even if this was another test.

I spotted Nora guards manning lookout stations. Each one held a gun that they hefted in their grips.

"You go!" shouted one, pointing his gun at the first Noir in the line.

When he didn't respond, the guard shot at his feet. The angel vaulted into the sky, only to scream when he fell down, his wings cracking as an invisible wire split through his feathers and left a trail of blood splattering across the ground. The guards quickly shot him with enough bullets to send feathers puffing into the air.

One down.

The intercom sounded again. "There is only one safe path. Fly wisely."

I swallowed hard as I realized this was very much a pass-fail type of training. Like with the arena, the Warden had decided to cull the herd.

Sorin grabbed my wrist hard enough to make my fingertips go numb. "You stay downwind," he bit out.

"I will do no such thing," I snapped back and launched into the air before he could stop me. My wings had been itching for flight ever since I got here, and I wasn't going to miss this opportunity, no matter what.

The Nora guards barked at the inmates to follow my lead and get flying before they rained bullets down on the crowd.

"Stupid female!" Zian shouted before I heard two heavy pairs of wings propelling male bodies into the air.

Sorin and Zian were on my tail—I felt their eyes on me—as were the other inmates who heeded the shots fired into the crowd.

I concentrated, spotting the translucent wire a fraction of a second before I dodged out of the way. As a female, my eyesight was better than the others'—a lot better. I might be small, but I had a few advantages over the brutish sex that they probably didn't know about.

Even with my keen eyesight, I missed one barb that managed to snag the tip of my left wing, making pain explode down my back as sensitive feathers were severed, but I corrected my course and kept going.

The first Noir had been aiming to fly directly upward, no doubt hoping to escape if he could get enough altitude. But I wasn't going to pretend to think I could escape so easily.

A platform rested on the opposite side of the yard, objectively smaller than the starting one. Surely the Warden expected a low pass rate.

With my target in mind, I hovered low, keeping the glare

of dying sunlight in my favor to spot any more of the barbed traps just before they clipped me.

My feet hit the platform, and I let out a breath. Safely on the other side, I watched my companions land and was met with an irritated Sorin, and Zian, who looked rather impressed. They might not have survived on their own, my path the correct one. Something the inmates behind them had caught on to as well as they followed our path up to the platform.

Then I saw the barbs move, and a wave of inmates went falling down onto the yard.

Bullets rained down after that.

As I watched the rest of the inmates struggle to make their way to safety, I knew this was only the beginning of the challenges we'd face at Noir Reformatory.

This place wasn't about reform at all.

It was about survival, and no matter what, I would make sure I was the last one standing.

CHAPTER FIVE

SORIN

I STOPPED COUNTING TIME when we reached nearly a decade in imprisonment. There wasn't a point.

Yet I ticked a seventh mark on the wall this morning, marking the days Zian and I had spent in captivity with Raven.

Why?

Because her scent was driving me mad and I needed the reassurance of time to remind myself why I hadn't touched her. I wasn't weak. Neither was Zian. But her citrusy aroma spiked more and more with each passing minute, her feminine call an intoxicating presence that allured every male in this fucking reformatory.

Including the Nora guards.

Zian and I were doing our best to protect her, which painted targets on our backs. Fortunately for her, we could handle it. But I suspected the guards would soon switch her bunking arrangements just to torment her.

And that would be a very bad day for the little dove because she didn't stand a chance against the monsters in this prison.

I rolled my neck as the doors opened, our afternoon time in the yard next on today's schedule. Zian led the way, Raven behind him and me at her back.

Those beautiful black plumes brushed my chest, causing me to wonder for the millionth time how such a delicate creature ended up here. I knew better than to ask. Raven wasn't a chatty female, preferring to show her teeth more than her voice, almost as if she grew up in this environment or something similar.

She possessed a sharp exterior, but she wore her true emotions in those big black eyes.

Eyes that were now taking in the yard and noting the subtle changes just like I was.

"Something's coming," she whispered.

"No shit," I agreed, spying the faint lines drawn into the ground.

More Noir arrived daily, fresh from the arena, filling our cells to near capacity again after the flying-lesson cull from the other day.

Which meant we were due for yet another party with death.

"What do you think?" Zian asked, his shoulder bumping mine as we surveyed the surroundings.

"Clearly not another flight test," I muttered, eyeing the barbwire above our heads.

"Dueling." Raven's soft voice shifted my focus to follow her gaze to where it rested on the ground.

"What?"

"It's set up like a duel," she explained, pointing to something my male eyes couldn't interpret. Eyesight enhancements were some of the female angels' strengths, while musculature and brute power belonged to the males.

Marking a duel as incredibly unfair to one in her position.

She could fight, her feet lithe, her body small, but she wouldn't stand a chance against any of the males in this place.

"I don't see it," Zian muttered. "Where are the lines?"

"It's more of those nearly invisible strands, like in the sky," she explained just as one of the inmates walked into one.

Electricity sizzled in the air, sending the Noir to his knees on a shriek of pain.

And another walked into the opposite side, joining the experience of his rival.

I hissed as the jolt of energy swirled, revealing the cylinder-shaped arena Raven's gaze had caught before ours. They formed tiny little cages meant for two bodies at most, clearly outlining today's cruel task.

A Nora guard confirmed it as he took the stage, telling us to divide into pairs for today's training exercise.

"Take Raven," Zian said. "I'll go play with our buddy Mandrin."

I snorted. *Mandrin* was absolutely not our buddy, the jackass Noir one of the inmates posing the biggest challenge to Raven. She had no idea, having not been privy to some of his crude remarks the other afternoon in the yard. We did our best to shield her, mostly on principle. Mandrin, however, possessed no manners or principles and would absolutely rape her repeatedly if given the chance.

"Kick his ass, Z."

"Oh, that's the plan." Zian cracked his neck and flashed a smirk at the tall jackass awaiting our challenge. We hadn't made our distaste a secret, and neither had he. "Here's your chance to prove your worth, big guy," Z taunted him. "If you're brave enough to take me on."

The giantlike asshole grinned wolfishly in welcome. "Bring it on, pixie legs."

I bit back a laugh, knowing the insult would only rile Zian up more. He might be on the leaner side, but that was what made him so quick on his feet. He was also solid muscle without an ounce of fat on him, making him strong, too.

Raven started to walk away, her intention of finding another sparring partner clear. I snagged the back of her neck and tugged her to me, our chests brushing from the roughness of my yank. "Stay."

"Fuck you."

"Later," I suggested, holding her with ease as she tried to wriggle out of my grasp. "Unless you want to spar naked in the ring, which I'll happily accommodate."

"I'm not partnering with you."

"You are absolutely partnering with me," I corrected, using my opposite arm to snag her waist. "I'm the only one here aside from Z who won't try to mount you afterward," I added against her ear. Then I spun her in my arms to show her the yard and force her to take in all the hungry stares. "Every single one of these guys wants a piece of you, little dove. Fighting will only exacerbate it. So accept my offer— it's your only intelligent option."

She bristled at that, then shivered as one of the males licked his lips while checking out her worn shirt. I knew from experience that the ratty thing was practically see-through, her rosy little buds a tempting outline that I dreamt of nightly.

"What will it be?" I asked her, aware of her body curling into mine rather than away from it. My scent seemed to wreak almost as much havoc on her as hers did on me, our bodies more than compatible for mating. It didn't matter that she was younger. Most female Nora mated around the age of nineteen or twenty, and typically to a group of much older male Nora. Some chose two mates, some more. It just depended on the bond cycle.

As a female coming of age, surrounded by two former warriors, it wasn't surprising our souls found the other intriguing.

But that didn't mean we had to act on it.

"Fine," she muttered. "I'll enjoy pushing you into that fence thing."

I dipped my head to her neck to nip her thundering pulse. "Is that why your heart is racing in fear right now?" I whispered. "Because you're worried I'll do that to you instead?"

"It's racing in anticipation, not fear."

"Sure," I returned. "If that thought makes you feel better, run with it."

She tried to twist away from me again, but I still had one arm wrapped around her, my opposite hand at her throat. It allowed me to hold her with ease, forcing her to watch as Zian and Mandrin stepped into the ring through a makeshift door the Nora had created for them. As soon as they were inside, they snapped it shut and electricity raced up the wires, locking them in.

"The rules are easy. First one to survive wins," the Nora announced as similar fence-like structures shot up from the ground, encircling all the pairs in the yard.

Including us.

I held on to Raven, the front of the wires whirring past my forearm to nearly burn my skin. One step forward and my little dove would have been skewered alive.

"Shit," she breathed, her heart truly scampering in terror now.

Meanwhile, the rule played over and over in my head. *First one to survive wins.* "This is a fight to the death," I breathed.

Sounds of violence and male grunts echoed through the air, threatening zaps of energy whizzing through my ears, and Raven's body began to shake against mine.

She didn't stand a chance, and we both knew it.

But that didn't mean she wouldn't go down without a proper fight, something she proved when she stomped on my foot unceremoniously.

I cursed but didn't release her, my grip on her throat tightening. "Stop. We need to think about this."

"Think about what?" she demanded, trying to escape my hold. "All you have to do is walk me forward and fry my brains!"

I yanked us both a step backward instead, the fence behind me allowing us about four more feet of maneuverability with a few additional feet on each side.

Not the ideal cage for a fight, making it very possible for both fighters to easily die against the electric currents. All it would take was a swift kick to send both bodies outward to connect the wings to the vibrating wires, and it'd all go to hell from there.

I pulled my feathers in as close to my body as possible, aware that my larger size made me more likely to touch the outside first.

Raven continued to try to free herself, causing me to tighten my grip. "Stop," I repeated, my voice a growl.

"Fuck you!" she shrieked, her trust issues on full display. Which, yeah, we barely knew each other. I understood that, but a week of protecting her should be worth some semblance of faith.

When her heel hit my shin this time, I bit down on her neck.

She screamed and started to fight in earnest.

Leaving me only one choice.

If she wasn't going to work with me to solve this, then I'd solve it myself.

Tightening my hold around her middle, I squeezed her throat tighter, blocking off her airway. She sputtered, her nails coming to my wrists to dig into them, to stop me from strangling her.

"I tried to work with you," I whispered against her ear. "You wouldn't listen. So I'm going to knock you out instead." *While I figure a way out of this mess*, I added to myself.

Her terror permeated the air, causing my heart to give a subtle pang in my chest. I didn't enjoy hurting her, not like this, but she refused to calm down. And after our little experience in the arena, I couldn't exactly rely on her not to stab me in the literal back.

She flailed.

A tear leaked down her cheek.

And she gave a silent whimper.

Meanwhile, I counted, my lips in her hair, my experience in chokeholds at the forefront of my mind. She'd be pissed when she woke up and would likely have a temporary sore throat, but she'd eventually see that this was the right thing to do.

Her body finally went limp, yet I waited an additional ten seconds, aware that she might be faking it. Then I gently led her to the gravelly earth below. When I stood back up, it was to find a furious Nora angel on the other side of our enclosure. "The fight is to the death," he snarled.

I gave him a bored look. "Then give me an opponent worthy of my strength."

"Kill her."

"Not in the mood," I drawled, crossing my arms. "So how about you come join me in here and we'll properly dance?"

He growled, causing two more Nora guards to hurry over to him, their white wings reminding me of a past I no longer dreamed about. My cravings to rejoin that world had died many decades ago, inspiring a vengeance inside that desired eventual retribution. If the three of them joined me now, I'd adore taking them down.

But instead, they did something to shrink our enclosure.

"Choose," one of the Nora demanded. "Either finish her or you both die."

My jaw ticked as I considered my options, aware that he would very likely follow through on his threat. Dying at the expense of some female didn't appeal to me. Yet my warrior sensibilities refused to be the one to snuff the life out of her.

So instead, I took a protective position over her, my feet straddling her slender waist as I folded my arms and glowered at the guards. "Do your worst."

They shared a sinister look, the cage closing in around me.

I feigned disinterest, attempting to call their bluff, when I sensed Raven stirring between my legs. She released a raspy gasp, her palm closing in around her freshly bruised throat.

That was fast, I acknowledged, surprised she recovered so quickly. It suggested she might have some sort of healing gift, something that was uncommon but not unheard of for females.

The wires hummed, reminding me of their nearness. We couldn't fight now even if we wanted to at this close range.

Raven yelped as one touched her foot, her knees tucking

up sharply and nearly knocking me off-balance.

But I remained standing, braced for impact.

"There's no honor in death," one of the Nora said. "Finish her and we'll spare you."

"No." Not only did I refuse to kill something so far below my strength, but I also didn't trust them to follow through. They'd probably let me fry at this point merely for amusement.

"What the fuck is going on over here?" a deep voice bellowed, a male without wings approaching with a cigarette hanging from his lips. He spat it out on the ground to stomp beneath one giant boot, his broad shoulders and tapered waist covered in a dress shirt, tie, and long leather coat that ended around his knees.

Definitely not a Nora.

A human, maybe?

The fence halted a few inches away from my wings, leaving me completely immobile. All it would take was a single shove from Raven, and I'd end up entangled and fried alive. But she smartly remained utterly still beneath me, perhaps because she realized the electricity could travel from me to her with a single touch.

Or maybe she'd finally learned to think before acting out.

Doubtful, I thought, observing the newcomer and memorizing his sharp traits. His dark hair was cropped close to his head, lending an edgy appeal that matched his rugged features. And his eyes were fathomless pits of cruelty.

"He's refusing to kill the female," one of them explained. "We told him it was either her life or both. He chose both."

The wingless male took in my stance and eyed Raven with interest between my legs. "Is she his mate?"

"No," all three guards said at once. "Just the only piece of ass in this sector of the prison."

Sector? I thought, curious. That implied there were additional sections. Which I already knew to be true considering Novak's disappearance, but the arrival of this new male—who displayed signs of being in charge—suggested there might be more to it than just a few additional Noir areas.

His cold gaze met mine, sending an icy shock through my system. Literally.

Not human, I decided immediately. *But definitely not Noir or Nora either.*

So what was he? Whatever he was, he seemed to lack a soul, because I caught nothing but death in his eyes.

"Open the cell," he demanded, confirming my suspicion about his superior position.

The Nora instantly obeyed, and the electric hum disappeared into the earth.

I didn't move. Neither did Raven. The newcomer's iron fist met my jaw, sending another of those frigid ice picks down my spine. Whatever he was, he oozed danger and had chosen me as a new target.

His other fist met my stomach, causing me to flinch.

But I didn't loosen my stance.

I could take a few hits, thanks to daily training with Zian and Novak. I was also smart enough not to hit back in this situation.

A hint of admiration mingled with annoyance in the wingless male's expression. He cocked his head and nodded at a nearby Nora. "Take him to Brina. She'll enjoy playing with this one."

She?

One of the Nora grabbed my arm, yanking me away from Raven.

"And the girl?" I heard another ask.

"Toss her back in her cell."

Relief touched me briefly at the knowledge that she'd be safe, until I caught Zian's livid expression on my way out. I tried to convey to him that this was my choice, that I'd be fine, but his pupils radiated murder.

The dead Noir at his feet seemed to be an omen for Raven's fate.

"Don't," I told him as we passed.

A sharp jab to my side quieted anything else I could say,

the guard having thought I meant the word in defiance. Rather than correct him, I followed in silence, down through a tunnel and into a portal of some sort.

One that opened to another area of the prison, through multiple doors and downward into yet another portal.

The scenery changed along the way, the structure of the reformatory seeming to morph to different climates until we reached a dark lair flickering with candlelight.

A female with bright red hair appeared, a scar over her left green eye. Lethality radiated from her despite her demure size. *Another being without wings*, I mused. *Fascinating*.

The scalpel in her hand, however, was not so intriguing.

"The Warden asked me to deliver a gift to you," the Nora said, shoving me forward, his dislike of the female palpable.

Her lips kicked up at the ends. "Ah, a Noir. I haven't had the pleasure yet of meeting one of these." She tucked that curtain of red hair behind her pointed ears, her pixie face beaming with excitement. "I hear you can take a lot of pain." She cocked her head. "Please tell the Warden I'll thank him later for the beautiful present."

"Gladly," the Nora replied, leaving us.

"Now, now, now, where to begin?" she hummed, dancing around me with her blade. "I know!"

She sliced the side of my wing, ripping the tendons straight off my shoulder and sending me to my knees on a groan I felt to my very soul.

Her responding laugh chilled me to the bone.

This woman is insane.

And they've just left me under her care.

Fuck.

CHAPTER SIX

RAVEN

JUST WHEN I THOUGHT I had Sorin figured out, he went and did some stupid shit like being the sacrificial hero.

Why would he do that?

It had to be some protective instinct that came with being a compatible mate, right?

And who the hell was that guy in the leather coat? Where were his wings? One of the Nora guards had addressed him as *Warden*, suggesting he owned this place. It'd been on the tip of my tongue to demand to know why I'd been sent here, only my throat still hadn't recovered from Sorin's manhandling.

Irritation tingled across my skin. Sure, I was grateful to be alive, but I didn't like that Sorin had saved me—again. Nor did I appreciate the manner in which he'd done it.

Confusion processed its way through my brain as a Nora guard bruised my arm while dragging me back to my cell. The guard seemed to be as annoyed with me as I was with my tattooed savior. It wasn't my fault that Sorin was stupid enough to defy the rules, but surviving never won me any favors with the local white-winged pricks. My mere ability to breathe seemed to annoy the crap out of them.

Being a Noir marked me as sinister and wrong.

The fact that I was a *female* Noir made it that much worse, as if I'd committed the ultimate sin just by existing.

"Get back in your cell," the guard barked with a sneer as he shoved me toward the bars that creaked open.

I nearly obeyed until I found Zian in there waiting for me. Somehow he'd beaten us back, and he looked ready to slaughter me.

"You can't leave me with him. Are you mad?" I screeched as I flapped my wings to put some distance between me and an enraged Zian. His dark hair was always a choppy hot mess around his face, but he looked particularly disheveled today, as if he'd been gripping at it. His dark eyes glimmered with madness as a cruel grin revealed deceptively sweet dimples.

The guard shoved me again, sending me stumbling forward into the cell. He slammed the bars closed before I had a chance to escape again. "You survived one fight to the death," he mused, grinning at my insane cellmate. "Let's see if you can do it again."

He walked off, and I spun around, shielding myself with my wings as I flattened against the cold bars. "Hey… Zian."

He ripped my wings aside, making me cry out as he broke sensitive feathers. His iron grip went straight for my already sore throat as he lifted me off my feet.

I winced, the pain from Sorin's earlier attack still fresh and embedded in my skin.

"Sorin should have killed you," he declared, his voice raw with rage. "First Novak, now Sorin. You know what I think? I think you enjoy toying with us while you play the innocent little dove." He growled as he leaned in, his breath hot on my face. "Did you know ravens are bad omens?" He squeezed, making my vision tinge black around the edges, just like before. "There's only one way to deal with omens. Snuff them out before they bring any further misfortune."

I clawed at his wrists, desperately trying to free myself, but from the sparring sessions I'd seen between Sorin and Z, I'd learned that pain was not the way to get through to this male. He blatantly ignored the streaks of blood left by my nails down his arms, so I went with the only tactic I had in my arsenal that seemed to affect him. I hadn't had time to try it on Sorin, not with an audience, but here in this cell that was permanently permeated with a pleasant scent, maybe I could pull it off.

I fluttered my eyes closed and concentrated. I thought of how he and Sorin fought, how they fucked, and how my need for them was bottled up inside me in a mixture of desire and hatred.

It worked.

Zian's nostrils flared and he let me go, sputtering as he slammed back into the bunk beds.

"Turn that off," he demanded as he swiped at his nose. "I don't want to smell you, you little bitch."

I grinned, because a puff of caramel sweetness tinged the air in response.

"Did you think you were teaching me a lesson every time you fucked around with Sorin in front of me?" I asked, growing bolder as I straightened. "The only lesson I learned was how to control my mate instincts." I'd remained deprived, while he always had Sorin to satisfy him. Without the tattooed warrior here to see to his needs, Zian would be at my mercy.

His dark eyes flared with danger. "You're playing with fire, Raven. This entire prison wants to fuck you enough already. Turn. It. Off. "

"Make me."

He launched forward, grabbing my throat yet again and pressing his lips dangerously close to mine. "Maybe I will *make you*, sweet bird. Maybe I'll mistake your scent as an invitation."

I swallowed, his heat seeping into my skin and forcing me to question my defensive move. "You won't," I whispered, more to reassure myself, not him.

"What makes you think that?" he asked, his smoldering

gaze searing mine.

"You've had a hundred chances to do so already and haven't." I practically choked on the words, his grip bruising me almost as badly as Sorin's had. But the statement felt true down to my very soul.

Zian and Sorin seemed to hold themselves to some unspoken code. They kept each other honest—at least, as honest as two hardened criminals could be. But if I'd learned anything from my time in captivity, it was that the worst of the worst lived by a code of loyalty and honor, and it was never broken. It was a risk to assume Zian and Sorin had such a pact, but this was my one card to play and I was going to go for it.

He bared his teeth at me and released me as suddenly as he'd grabbed me, this visceral, primal side of him making my feathers spike. I was flirting with a savage fate, but as he paced around me like a caged animal, I knew I'd guessed right.

"There are other ways to find release," he said as he resumed a fighting stance, flaring his wings out to give himself balance. "I've been wanting a go at you ever since I saw you fight in the arena. Let's see what you've got."

He lunged for me, which wasn't Zian's typical go-to move. He exercised patience and precision in battle, but now he blindly threw himself at me.

Big mistake.

I flicked my wings to propel myself out of the way, my small stature making it easy to trade brute force for speed. Zian had probably never fought a female, and even if he had decades of training on me, he wasn't thinking straight.

A light push was enough to redirect him straight into the bars. His momentum sent him hard into the metal, creating a *ping* that resounded throughout the cell. He grunted, stunned, before turning and launching himself at me again.

Would he never learn?

Using the same tactic, I sent him sprawling into the bunk beds, leaving a large dent in one of the poles as it gave under his weight. Except this time he'd expected the ploy, and I shrieked as I found myself yanked to the ground by my ankle.

"Never use the same strategy twice in a row," he chided, climbing on top of me in an instant and pinning me to the ground. He pressed his thighs into mine, making me gasp at the intimate pain as his hips dug into mine. I went still as he leaned in and snarled.

It was a stupid move, but I'd been cooped up with two insanely hot angels and a fog of need ever since I'd arrived here.

I purred.

His pupils blew wide when the rumble went through his chest. "S-stop that," he stuttered.

Squirming underneath him, I intensified the intimate sound. I'd heard females do it before, but I'd never tried it myself. It was typically reserved for mates, although I had no idea what it might do to a compatible male.

His entire body trembled, and his jaw worked as he visibly restrained himself. From fucking me or killing me, I wasn't sure.

A chittering came from the crack in the wall, and I realized that Mousey Mouse had been watching the show. His mind brushed mine, horrified that I was about to die just when he'd come to tell me the news that my tattooed tormentor had been taken to the underground bad place to be tortured by some insane doctor.

"What?" I asked it, confused by the description. "What doctor?"

"Who are you talking to?" Zian demanded.

"Shh," I whispered, focused on Mousey Mouse. It gave me a name I didn't recognize. "Brina?"

Zian arched a brow, and I met his gaze, my purring long gone.

"Mousey Mouse says Sorin has been taken to a dungeon to be tortured by some crazy doctor named Brina."

His brow furrowed. "You can communicate with that thing?"

"Yeah."

"And you're just telling me this now?"

"You haven't been all that chatty yourself," I snapped, trying to wiggle out from beneath him.

But he refused to give me an inch of space. "Ask it where Novak is."

"Let me go and I'll consider it."

"Do it and I'll release you."

I ground my teeth, considering my options. Then sighed when I realized I really didn't have one. So I turned to Mousey Mouse and asked about Novak. He chittered back at me, saying he didn't know, so I had Zian describe him.

"Dark hair, ice-blue eyes, similar build to mine, black wings. He won't be speaking. He also might try to eat your new pet."

I didn't relay that last part to Mousey Mouse but did suggest he give Novak a wide berth and not try to engage him. With a little squeak, he disappeared into the wall, and I looked at the male on top of me. "Satisfied?"

"Hardly," he muttered.

But he did get off of me.

And proceeded to ignore me for the rest of the night.

CHAPTER SEVEN

ZIAN

NINE NIGHTS WITHOUT NOVAK.

Two without Sorin.

All of them stuck in a cell with a little birdlike creature with big doe eyes and lips made for sin.

I glared at the ceiling, trying not to think about those damn lips wrapped around my hard cock. Trying and *failing*. It was that damn purr from the other night, the arousing sound I couldn't seem to forget. The hypnotic noise haunted my fucking dreams, making me hate her even more.

Which only increased my desire to fuck her with each passing minute.

I pinched the bridge of my nose, my opposite hand going to my dick to give it a firm stroke. Because, yeah, I was naked. And I didn't care if she could see me. It would serve her right for putting me in this damn position.

She knew, too.

I could *smell* her interest because she was just as awake as I was, her pussy permeating our room with a sweet mating aroma.

Last night, I demanded she shut it off, which only made it worse.

It seemed the sweet bird enjoyed being bossed around. Or maybe it was the art of rebellion she favored. I couldn't tell, but if she didn't cut that shit out soon, she'd earn my wrath in the form of a harsh fuck against the bars of the cell door.

Unfortunately, the claim would only increase the interest of the males in the reformatory, each one wanting a pass at the ripe female Noir.

Meaning I had no real reason to fuck her other than to cool my own need.

And that was unacceptable.

Yet provided one hell of a fantasy escape in my mind.

I swallowed a groan as I pictured her legs around my waist, her slick cunt taking me deeper and deeper with each thrust. She'd moan, both from pleasure and pain, as I pinned her against the metal bars with my hips.

Harder and harder.

Drawing blood because I could.

Mmm, the image was perfection. Her pant in my ear, mingled with a cry as I bit down on her neck, made me smile. It wasn't real, but it *felt* real. The desire to thoroughly take her, both in spirit and in body, drove my hand up and down my shaft, over and over again, pumping my pleasure to new heights.

I wanted her beneath me. On the ground. Pounding her into the cement floor, punishing her for taking Sorin away. For enraging Novak. For being the reason they were both gone.

Not rational or true, but it didn't fucking matter in my mind. I was the master of my fantasies, and in this one, she was to blame for every damn thing going wrong. I took her with a fervor, not stopping when she begged me to slow down, instead pushing her more and loving the way she cried out in violent pleasure.

Because that was how we would fuck.

It'd be a savage mixture of rapture and agony.

She'd take it because I'd make her take it.

And then she'd thank me afterward as she lay replete on the floor, our joint arousal painting her pussy lips and thighs.

I nearly came from the vision alone, my inhales escalating as my heart pounded against my ribs.

"Zian," I heard her whisper below, her small frame so close and panting with need. "What are you doing?"

"Fuck off," I muttered, not wanting to spoil the moment with her innocent questions. The guards had purposely put us in a cage together, knowing we would be compatible. It was only a matter of time before one of us caved. I suspected they wanted us to mate, if anything to rip the other away and perform unspeakable torment on the pair.

I wouldn't succumb to that.

Refused to tie myself so completely to another.

Novak and Sorin were my only family. I didn't need or desire anyone else, no matter how alluring a fuck could be to my sex-deprived form.

Oh, Sorin satisfied me plenty.

But there was something about a soft, pliant female that I both craved and missed. Having one so close, one who seemed to be aching for me almost as badly as I ached for her, only made it that much harder to stay away.

Hating her helped.

Except deep down I knew it wasn't her fault at all that Sorin had chosen to protect her over himself. Because I would have done the same damn thing in his shoes.

Hence my irrational distaste of the female. She created a weakness none of us could afford. She needed to go. Yet I had nowhere to send her because I couldn't stand the thought of another Noir getting his hands on her.

She wouldn't last a day in another cell.

The monsters here had no morals or warrior codes.

They were true terrors, pulled from the worst Noir prisons throughout the system. Handpicked by *The Dark*

One himself, if the rumors were to be believed.

I shivered, my palm slowing against my cock.

This is wrong.

I can't do this.

I should—

Raven whimpered, our cell radiating lust in a dangerous way. Fuck, this had to be driving the other inmates crazy. They'd want to take her even more tomorrow, meaning I would have a lot of protecting to do.

Again.

I nearly growled, my frustration over this situation mounting my arousal that much more. Because how the fuck did I become her guardian? Why?

Because no one else will do it.

Because she'll suffer without you.

Because she'll probably die swiftly otherwise.

Maybe that would be best for her. This place wasn't meant for sweet little birds like Raven. This time I snarled, the thought of her expunged life pissing me off.

Females were rare.

They should be cherished.

"You shouldn't fucking be in this place," I snapped out loud. "Why are you here?" I rolled off my bunk, not caring at all that I wore nothing but my feathers.

Raven scurried back into her little hole, her wings flying around her in that protective manner she favored. "Zian," she breathed, her dark eyes drinking their fill of my nude form.

I ignored her virginal reaction and crouched before her. "Tell me how you gained your wings." I didn't want to guess. I didn't want to beat around the bush. I wanted to know. I had a fucking right *to know* as her protector. "What did you do to get sent here?"

"I was born," she whispered.

I waited for more, but she said nothing else. "And then?" I prompted, not really desiring a life story but needing a bit more than her damn creation.

"That's it." She visibly shivered. "I was born with black wings."

My eyebrows shot up. "That's impossible." All angels were born with white wings. The Nora only turned Noir when they Fell, which was marked by black feathers. Unless Novak's little tale from long ago was actual true. But yeah, I highly doubted that rogue Noir actually existed.

Besides, Raven had to know how Noir were made already, which implied she was fucking with me. I reached for her in her false haven, grabbed a handful of her feathers, and yanked her out of her little hole.

She yelped as she landed unceremoniously on her ass beside me. I stood, towering over her. "Let's try this again, sweet bird. Tell me how you gained your wings."

"I was born with them!" she insisted, her tone angrier than before.

Which only made me harder.

The thought of fucking her into submission turned me on far too much.

I really should have finished the task of jacking off *before* touching her.

"That's—"

"Impossible," she finished for me, shooting up to a fighting stance. "Yeah, I know. But it doesn't make it any less true." Her hands were lifted in the air as if ready to take me on.

I studied her posing, noting the weakness of her posture. She was conflicted, as if part of her wanted to battle me while the other part had already conceded.

What would she do if I crowded her against the wall, wrapped my palm around her throat, and kissed her? Would she bite me? Would I bite her back? *Oh, yes, no question.* I could already taste her blood on my tongue, the flavor addicting and ripe and so very female.

"You're scaring me," she whispered.

"Good." She should be frightened. Because I was the only one standing between her and a dozen or so inmates who wanted a piece of her. "Go to bed, Raven."

"I was trying to sleep. You ripped me out of my bunk."

"And I'm giving you the opportunity to return to your false safe haven. I suggest you take it. Now."

She swallowed, her arms beginning to shake as she took a step around me, her big black eyes guarded and watchful. I didn't grab for her, so she inched closer to her bed and was about to slip inside when a foreign stench swirled around us.

I glanced toward it just as a sharp pang hit my side, slicing through my skin. Screams and shouts rent the air throughout the reformatory, my own lips parting on a gasp at the agonizing sensation shredding my torso.

My knees gave out beneath me, the shock of being *stabbed* momentarily stunning me into submission.

"What the fuck!" Raven shouted, her wings beating around us in a flurry of black feathers. She moved with a speed I would have admired had my mind been functioning properly.

A dark, angelic knight riding to my rescue.

Except that wasn't it at all.

She yanked the object out of my side, leaving me on the floor as she squared off with the figment in our cell. I collapsed on my back, my breaths uneasy, my vision blurring.

Until a giant, four-eyed *thing* crept into my vision. *The fuck is that?* I thought, unsure if I was dreaming this all up or not. I certainly felt delirious enough for this to be a messed-up nightmare.

Yet I'd never envision Raven taking something like that on by herself.

She moved with the grace of a feline cat, her feet quick over the floor as she slashed at the wide, slobbering mess of a thing. "Don't you dare," she said to it.

The creature snarled in response.

"Well, I don't care if you want to eat him. I said no."

My eyes widened. *Yeah, this has got to be a dream.* Because no way in hell would someone who was sane try to hold a conversation with a ghastly being like that.

"Don't make me do this," she continued, sounding regretful. "Just disappear. Go back to wherever you came from."

I blinked at her as if she were the monster, not the

seven-foot, creepy shithole before her.

Why am I still on the floor? I palmed my side. *Oh, right. So that's still real.*

Raven made a noise that sliced through my heart, part sad, part anger. "No."

No what? I wondered, prodding at the deep wound in my side. Not fatal or anything that would keep me down too long, but enough to nearly puncture my lungs, which explained my faltering vision and harsh breaths.

Fortunately, I healed quickly.

A screech preceded the creature's movement, followed by a shout from Raven as she ran forward and plunged the blade-like thing into the four-eyed beast's chest. My heart raced as the two of them grappled, the slimy being's body dwarfing hers by several feet.

But whatever she'd done with that dagger seemed to be a deadly injury, the nightmare beginning to writhe and shrink before us until all that remained was a puddle of black ooze.

I gaped at it as Raven fell to her knees beside me, her palms on my torso, searching as she fretted over my injury.

It took me a moment to realize she was speaking to me, her tone filled with concern. *Concern for me.*

"I'm fine," I managed to say, my voice far more hoarse than it should be.

She shook her head, her nimble fingers pulling my hands away. I tried to cover the wound again, only to be hissed at and shoved down to my back. If this were a proper dream, I'd grab her and roll her beneath me.

Except she remained in charge, her palm covering my wound and singeing my skin. *Literally.*

"What are you...?" I trailed off, the zap of energy migrating up my side leaving me warm and oddly soothed. *Healing,* I realized numbly. *She's healing me.*

A rare Nora gift.

One only females possessed, mostly as a result of their need to heal themselves. They were so unique and outnumbered that it made sense to be born with a natural defense. But to use it on another was even more unusual.

Especially to gift a non-mate with such a sensation.

I tried again to pull her away, not appreciating the intimacy of her touch. Or perhaps appreciating it too much.

She easily overpowered me, suggesting I was in a much worse state than I understood. *This could still be a dream*, I mused, blinking as black dots danced around my head. They eventually cleared to reveal the ceiling. Then the top of a bunk. I frowned, uncertain of how or when that changed.

Something soft curled into my side, a black wing cradling my chest.

What the hell?

I looked down to find Raven using my shoulder as a pillow, her palm still pressed to my side.

She'd passed out during her energy transfer, her clammy skin suggesting she'd overexerted herself in the process. Now she lay vulnerable against my still-naked form, her delicate wing haphazardly strewn across my torso.

I ran my fingers through the soft feathers, considering her story about being born this way. Most Noir boasted about their past, unrepentant for their Fall. Not Raven. She seemed almost annoyed by the question, like she was asked frequently and constantly received a similar response to mine.

Was it possible that she spoke the truth? I traced the edge of her wing to her shoulder and then down her arm to the hand hovering over my healed wound. The skin felt smoother than silk beneath her touch, my insides functioning as expected.

The dagger she took from that thing must have possessed magical properties to cause so much damage with a single puncture. Somehow she'd known. Had I been worse than I realized? Given my lapse of time and understanding, it was possible.

Which meant she might have just saved my life at the expense of her own safety. Because I could do anything I wanted to her now as she rested against me. For some reason, that only made me want to protect her more.

I wrapped my arms around her, holding her in what I

now realized was *her* bed.

After everything I'd said and done to her, she'd chosen to help me. To save me. To heal me. The least I could do was guard her in return.

We didn't have to like each other to work together to survive. Tonight proved that.

I kissed the top of her head, the gesture natural. A thank-you of sorts. And a promise of a new alliance. It'd be tentative at best, but better than nothing. "I'll protect you, sweet bird," I whispered, aware she couldn't hear me. "Consider that my gift to you to show my gratitude."

A new bridge had formed between us.

We'd see how long it took before we burned it to the ground.

Chapter Eight

RAVEN

ZIAN SCRATCHED ANOTHER MARK on the wall, and the grating sound went right through my teeth down to my bones. He'd picked up the annoying habit after Sorin's relocation, although why they wanted to track how long we were in this hellhole, I had no idea. I wanted to tell him to knock it the fuck off, that it didn't matter if we were here for days or years because it all felt the same, but the brute loved it when I tried to boss him around.

We both knew he could have me flat on my back in an instant in any way he desired.

The fact that he hadn't was both comforting and agonizing.

Nearly three weeks in this cell together with the sexual tension rubbing us raw was starting to make me ache all over. I couldn't imagine what it was doing to Z. Given the amount of *rubbing* he did to himself—whether I was watching or not—suggested he was barely keeping his shit together as well.

Oh, and I *always* watched.

Resisting him would have been easier if he was his usual asshole self, but after saving his life against the ooze monster—whom I now called Mister Slobs—and healing him from his fatal wound, something had changed between us. I was used to fending for myself, building alliances that I could control, and never trusting anyone for longer than it suited me. Yet it wasn't like that with Zian.

Sure, he blamed me for Novak and he hated me for Sorin.

However, in spite of all that, I sensed some sort of developing camaraderie between us as I gripped the iron bars of our cell door, feeling his eyes on me, ever watchful, ever protective.

Pretending not to notice him, I peered into the gray-stoned corridor at the addition of more cellmates bloodied and stunned from the arena. We'd fallen into an endless cycle with the weekly culling and refilling of the cells with new meat.

"Remind me of today's itinerary, Rave," Zian said as he jumped off of his bunk, his lithe movements barely making a sound.

The new nickname made me tick my lips up. I continued peering down the hallway so he couldn't see how it pleased me. "It's workout day today." Our days had evolved to have an illusion of choice. Now, after breakfast, inmates could choose time in the yard or hit up the poor excuse for a gym. More like an indoor extension of the yard with oversized rocks that we were allowed to lift.

I secretly loved our workout days because Zian deemed I needed to be trained. It was the only reason I had survived the past two dueling matches, using his tactics to send my opponents into the electrified barriers before they could get their hands on me.

My skin tingled at the thought of sparring with him again. I'd seen how his sparring sessions always ended with Sorin, and I felt the same building heat each time we fought. I was getting better, and his approval was my secret drug, something I thrived off of in this otherwise nightmarish hellhole. Not because I needed it from him, but because I knew he was one of the most skilled warriors I'd ever seen in action. Survival was all that mattered in Noir Reformatory, and if I could learn how to fight, maybe, just maybe I could live long enough to figure out how to escape this place.

He hummed in response, and the low vibration made me want to purr again, but I resisted the sudden urge. Zian had already rubbed one out today, and breakfast was in a few minutes. With the changes to the schedule, including the nightly ooze-monster attacks, breakfast no longer boasted a line for food because only half of the inmates would get to eat—a fact the new additions would have to learn fast.

I flinched when Zian's wing faintly brushed mine. My feathers were incredibly sensitive, and I suspected he knew that. He flashed me a grin when I shyly glanced at him. "You never miss a thing, do you, sweet bird?"

I wasn't sure if he was referring to the attention I paid to our schedule or the fact that I'd felt his advance, however subtle. Opting for ignorance, I shrugged. "If you say so."

He crossed his arms and leaned against the bars. "I was impressed with your takedown on last night's monster," he said. "You killed it before I even got off my ass."

My feathers puffed out of their own accord before I could rein them back in. It was stupid, but I liked it when Zian complimented me. "It was my turn on watch," I reminded him. "Plus, Mousey Mouse gave me a heads-up this time."

His lips twitched. "Is that so? Well, I guess I'm glad Novak didn't eat him."

"Only because those batshit crazy demons he's trapped with distracted him." Poor Mousey Mouse had been kind enough to spy on the *Pereo Unit*—a fancy term for *solitary*—where Novak was being kept. The mouse had given us reports every other day for the last three weeks, assuring us that both of Zian's friends were still alive.

Novak seemed to be faring better than Sorin, a spell the

only danger to his existence at the moment. Well, that and the four psychotic demons housed in solitary with him. Fortunately, they were more focused on ripping the skin off some female, only intruding on Novak's space when they needed his cell to think.

Mousey Mouse said something about how the wards were less potent in Novak's area. I didn't quite follow, my concern more for Sorin after learning about his placement with an insane doctor.

The things she's doing to him... A shudder traversed my spine; just the thought was enough to churn my insides.

I hadn't repeated all the things Mousey Mouse had said about Sorin's predicament, mostly because I couldn't stomach it. I also didn't want to set Zian off, as things between us were going well and a selfish part of me didn't want to disturb the balance.

Zian's wing brushed mine again as he grinned, making guilt sting in my chest. I wanted to turn to him, tell him everything, and give my body to him as punishment.

Because, oh, I knew he would punish me in a brutal, beautiful way.

The cell doors opened, and I propelled myself through the entrance, grateful for the excuse to get away from Zian before I acted on my impulses. This was the one time he allowed me a hint of freedom. We needed to keep our strength up, which meant we needed to eat every single day, no matter how challenging they made it for us.

I might not have brute strength, but I had speed. My midnight hair flung behind me as I dashed down the corridor and past inmates who hurried toward the same goal. The new recruits blinked at us with confusion, still looking weary from surviving their orientation. If any of them were smart, they'd follow the herd.

Male hands grabbed at me, but I altered my course like Zian had taught me, moving too fast to be yanked down. Although, if any succeeded, Zian would eat their hearts for breakfast instead of whatever disgusting leftovers they had out for us today.

The doors rose along the far wall, revealing a table with

plastic-wrapped packages that would have a small portion of food. I buzzed to the closest end and grabbed two, whirling to head back to our cell. There were tables around the small courtyard, but no one ate at them unless they wanted to get jumped.

In my hurry, I didn't notice that a group had followed me, and I ran right into a hard chest, thumping onto the ground in a flurry of black feathers as I twisted my ankle. I hissed with pain, wanting to heal myself but knowing I couldn't show that particular skill out in the courtyard.

"How sweet of you to get me a package," said one of the Noir with a crooked nose that must have been broken one too many times to heal in such a way. He knelt and yanked one of my breakfast packages from my grip, then looked down at my breasts as if he was reconsidering his interest in food.

A shout made him change his mind, and he used his wings to launch away from me, taking the meal with him. "The heart-eater is coming!" came the warning.

Yeah, Zian loved that nickname, and he reminded me of it constantly.

He growled, showing teeth as he caught up with me. He glanced between the retreating Noir and me, clearly debating if he should pursue my attacker. At the risk of being left alone and likely losing yet another meal or worse, I was glad he opted to stay. He offered me a hand and I took it, electricity zinging up my arm at the contact.

By the way he flexed his jaw, I guessed he could feel it, too.

"I didn't see the bastard in time," I said as I shoved the meal at him and ducked my head. "Here, take it." He was my only protection, and I knew it. Not only did he need to keep his strength up, but I had to find a way to stay valuable to him if I wanted to survive. I wasn't going to pretend to think that this newfound friendship we had with one another was going to last forever.

He pushed the meal into my chest. "Hold on to it," he said, his tone leaving no room for debate as he guided me back to our cell, me limping against him as we went. He glared at anyone who came within touching distance, showing teeth when they didn't back away fast enough.

Because, yeah. They'd all seen Zian in the last two dueling matches. He'd made a show of it, ripping his opponents into pieces and eating their hearts just to make a point.

Hence, *heart-eater*.

When we returned to the cell, Zian forced me to consume the contents of the package, and I did as he commanded in silence. After I was done, I healed my ankle. It was a lot easier to do with a full stomach, but his generosity only made my guilt ping harder.

When he found out how bad Sorin had it because he'd spared me, I had a feeling our friendship would come to a screeching halt.

He kicked away my empty meal and jerked his chin toward the doorway. "Time for our workout."

I gave him a raised brow. "You sure you don't want to swap out today with intel-gathering at the yard?" So far we'd found out that a new crew was coming, one that would mix up the current hierarchy that might kick Zian off the top. We needed to figure out who was coming and get an edge.

He shook his head. "Nope. Today just proved that you have a long way to go. Getting your breakfast taken like a fledgling? It's embarrassing, Raven."

My fingers curled into fists, and I resisted the sudden urge to punch him in the face—not that I'd stand a chance. "Fine. Let's go."

We walked in silence to the makeshift gymnasium, both of us stopping when we noted that something was off.

I didn't have time to put my finger on it because a Noir was being led in by two Nora guards.

"Sorin," Zian said under his breath, the word a prayer.

Sorin was back.

And he looked like hell turned over.

Just in time for the alarms to blare overhead and a Nora guard to demand we all head out to the yard.

Zian and I shared a look, aware that this command

didn't match the predefined schedule for today.

Something's up, his eyes seemed to tell me.

I know, I agreed.

Sorin was already heading that way, never once looking in our direction, perhaps because he hadn't seen us. Or maybe he was eager to comply because he didn't want to take another beating. His wings certainly couldn't handle it, the fragments of feather and bone sticking out at awkward angles. He also appeared lost in his thoughts, something Zian seemed to notice as he glanced warily at me.

Did he know I kept this from him? That I knew about Sorin's state? Would he hold it against me?

A secondary alarm screeched through the reformatory, signifying an event.

This can't be good.

And worse, I might have just lost my one and only ally in this place.

CHAPTER NINE

SORIN

I CAN'T CATCH A FUCKING BREAK. That bitch Brina had done a number on my wings, leaving me broken in ways I hadn't felt in ages.

All in the name of "science."

Such bullshit.

She was a sadist with a scalpel and a deceptively sweet smile. I wanted to kill her more than I'd ever desired to kill anyone.

And Raven was second on my list.

Had I just strangled her in that damn duel, I never would have met the vile fae physician with a penchant for ripping her subjects apart.

"You Noir are new to my playground," she'd mused. *"Let's see how much pain you can handle. Oh! And how fast you can heal, too! This is going to be so much fun, darling. You'll see."*

I shuddered, my feathers shifting in agony as we stepped out into the courtyard. The wire nets were gone, replaced by sky-high platforms large enough for one or two Noir, max.

Great.

My wings were in no condition to fly, let alone play another elimination game.

This would be a true fight to the death—*my* death.

"Something isn't right," Zian said quietly as he lightly bumped my shoulder with his, a proper greeting between us unnecessary after a century of friendship. I also wasn't exactly in a talkative mood at the moment, more of a leave-me-the-fuck-alone-while-I-nap kind of frame of mind.

Raven came up to his other side, her wing brushing his in an odd show of solidarity that had me narrowing my gaze. *What happened while I was gone?* I wondered, my eyebrow inching upward when Zian absently returned the gesture.

"It's not time for another elimination day," he continued, surveying the crowd. "But it's not flying day either."

I frowned. "There's a daily itinerary?"

"You have no idea," he muttered, running his fingers through his hair. "It's more of a week—"

A spike shot up from the ground, inches from my face, sending the three of us upward on instinct. I winced as my shoulder blades cried out in pain, my broken bones not yet healed from Brina's most recent torture session.

Was that this morning?

I couldn't remember.

Nor did I have time to contemplate it as more spikes sprang up from the ground, some of them spearing Noir who hadn't taken off fast enough.

There was enough space between them to land, but I had to find a…

I squinted at the metal shards dotting the ground, my lips flattening. *Shit.* They'd begun to move in a pinwheel-like motion, creating a makeshift grinder for anyone falling out of the sky.

Awesome. Land and you'll be shredded, I realized. *Fuckers.*

"Oh, shit," Raven breathed.

"What do you see, Rave?" Zian asked, his focus intent.

Rave? I repeated to myself. *Really?*

"More of those invisible wires from the other week," she replied, giving me an idea of how long I was gone. If she meant the day we followed her upward, then I hadn't been in Brina's clutches for nearly as long as I'd thought. "We need to be careful on our ascent up to the plat—"

A Noir shrieked above, cutting off her comment, his body tumbling through the air and heading directly for me. I dove to the left, my wings immediately protesting the motion and causing me to do a backward somersault instead of an executed dive. Flailing in the wind, I managed to snap out my wings to steady myself about five feet above my death.

Warm liquid bathed my face as the Noir who nearly slammed into me hit the spikes, his fate sealed in a single swipe.

"Damn," I muttered, swallowing shallowly. My entire back spasmed as I tried to right myself to fly upward.

"You look like shit," Zian said, joining me and grabbing my elbow to yank me upward.

"Thanks. I feel like it, too." To the point where I worried about how long I could keep myself in the air.

Raven grasped my opposite elbow, sending a zap of unwanted electricity up my arm. I shook her off on instinct, sending her sideways. She spun a little, her balance faltering as she nearly face-planted into the makeshift grinder.

I cringed, an apology on the tip of my tongue, when fire whizzed through the air, grazing my wing. A curse left my mouth instead, my feathers immediately retreating into my body and sending me another foot lower.

My eyes screwed shut, my doom imminent, only I somehow remained airborne.

Because Zian has a hold on my arm.

"Don't you fucking give out on me now, asshole," he snapped in my ear, giving me a sharp yank upward. "I've put too much into this relationship to lose you to a damn shredding machine."

"Dick," I grumbled, flaring out my wings again and trying futilely to fly. "If you kill yourself by trying to save my ass, I'm haunting you in the afterlife."

"Will you two stop bickering and focus?" Raven snapped, taking my other arm in a tighter grip this time. "Don't you dare push me again," she added, her dark gaze capturing mine. "You saved my life. Now I'm going to save yours. Whether you like it or not."

Any other day, I might have laughed at that.

But another fireball whizzed past us, sobering me instantly.

"Where to?" Zian asked, his attention on Raven.

"There," she said, gesturing to a platform with her chin. Two Noir already took up the platform, their expressions fierce. "It's the closest one and has the least number of barbs."

"Making it the most popular location and it's already taken," Zian pointed out, even as we began our ascent.

"Yeah, so I hope you're in a fighting mood, because it's our only option with Sorin in tow." She tightened her grasp on me, her smaller wings beating twice as hard as she tugged me higher into the air. "It's the only platform with a wide enough circumference for us to fit through. Together."

Meaning we would be zapped if we tried to approach any of the others, and her small frame probably couldn't take the hit with her dragging my heavy ass up with her.

"I'm in the mood to fight," I said, meaning it. Just because I couldn't really fly didn't mean I couldn't throw a punch.

Zian snorted but said nothing as he used his much stronger wings to help us soar upward.

I attempted to assist, but my battered feathers screamed in agony each time I tried, the movement sending shock waves of pain down my spine. Brina had definitely done a number on me, and that fireball hadn't helped.

If we didn't take that platform, I was a dead Noir.

Adrenaline pumped through my veins, the last vestiges of my sanity urging me upward and preparing me mentally for what we needed to do.

Kill.

Raven reached the top first, her citrusy perfume blasting through the air in a current that stole my breath and ability to think. *What the—*

Her fist slammed into the first Noir's groin as her feet touched the ground, the male barking out a harsh insult in response while his buddy danced forward for his turn.

She ducked, maneuvering out of his reach while Zian yanked me upward. "Hold on and don't let go."

I grabbed the ledge, my body dangling haphazardly over the side as he hoisted himself up to join Raven, his expression a mixture of annoyance and pride.

My wings beat at my back, doing the bare minimum of helping me up while the other two fought for purchase on the platform from the air, their feathers in much better shape.

One of the Noir started toward me, his boots intent on smashing my fingers, but Raven blocked him and showered us both in her addictive scent.

He swayed a little, his lips pulling into a snarl as he lunged for her. "Come here," he demanded.

But she sent her knee upward into his sternum as she flexed her wings in a skilled maneuver I recognized from my early training days.

She's been practicing with Zian.

While impressive, it wasn't enough for the much larger Noir's size. He had her pinned against the pole a second later, his aggression painting a wave of intent in the air.

And Zian was too busy dealing with the other guy to help.

Which left me.

Stealing a deep breath, I coached myself into motion. *Just another pull-up, except with a bunch of dead weight on my back. Easy.*

But it wasn't easy at all.

It fucking hurt, and I nearly lost my grip halfway up. My legs swung beneath me, kicking at air, my shoulders heaving with pain. This should be a walk in the park, but all those drugs Brina had pumped me with still rioted in my veins. Not to mention the other unspeakable shit she did to my—

Raven squealed above, the Noir cupping her breast and squeezing way too tight. "You doused me in your scent, bitch. That's a fucking invitation."

She snarled something in reply, but I couldn't hear it over the roar of wind assaulting my ears as I yanked myself upward onto the platform. Only my toes fit on the edge, but it was enough for me to teeter forward, grab the Noir by his nape, and yank him backward off Raven.

She shoved forward at the same time, using her wings against the pole as leverage, and bounced upward to kick the guy in the head, her foot cracking so sharply across his jaw that it knocked him out.

His weight fell on me, causing me to lose my balance and sending me spiraling off the platform.

Only to be caught a second later by the waist of my pants.

Raven gave a little grunt as she tugged me upward in the air, her wings flapping furiously at her back. "Come on, Sorin. Use what's left of your feathers. Do it now."

Not having any choice, I flared my plumes outward, the broken shards barely working, but it was enough to force us upward a few feet and back onto the solid floor.

I collapsed in a pant, my back heaving from the effort, my body rushing hot and cold from the workout. Raven left me to help Zian finish off the other guy, their movements blurring before my eyes.

Dead weight, I thought glumly. Never had I left Zian to fight a battle for me, and I didn't appreciate the feeling.

Weakness wasn't something I understood.

But that fucking sadist had ruined me.

She'd tried to saw my damn wings off near the base, just to see if they would grow back. Thankfully, the Warden stepped in at that point and told her the experiment broke some sort of standards.

I nearly laughed.

This reformatory had *standards*.

Yeah. Right.

I coughed, my chest throbbing with the movement. My eyes felt heavy, as did all my limbs. *I just need a fucking nap.*

"Can you heal him?" Zian asked, his hand suddenly on my arm.

I blinked up at him, confused by how and when he'd landed beside me.

Then I realized my surroundings had subtly changed.

We were back in the cell.

"How…?" The word left my mouth without sound, my association with reality swaying in and out of focus.

"Yeah," Raven said, her hands on my bare chest. "But it's going to take a lot more energy than the Mister Slobs incident."

Mister Slobs? Am I dreaming?

"I have your back, sweet bird," Zian said softly, his wing brushing hers. "Just tell me what you need. And don't overdo it."

Yeah, I'm totally dreaming. Because Z was not the coddling type. Ever.

Raven nodded, her eyes falling closed as a warming sensation tingled across my skin. I flinched away from it, only to have Zian grab my shoulders and snap, "Stay still. She's helping you."

A too-quiet growl filtered from my chest, the sound weak and disoriented.

Zian snorted in response. "Just take it, Sorin. We both know you're good at that."

My jaw clenched. If I could speak, I'd tell him what I'd like to take right about now. But as Raven's foreign touch worked itself through my system, I found myself less and less tense and a hell of a lot warmer.

"She's good, isn't she?" Zian murmured, his hands massaging my shoulders now.

I grunted, wanting to neither confirm nor deny his statement. Yet I closed my eyes and just allowed myself to *feel*.

This was likely a dream, and I'd wake tomorrow on Brina's lab table again.

So I'd enjoy the tender sensations of Raven's touch and Zian's knowing hands while I could.

It might be my last date with happiness for a while.

CHAPTER TEN

RAVEN

I SHOULD HAVE FELT COLD. Every time I woke up in this horrible place, my nose ached. I only had my feathers to hold in the scant warmth created by my petite frame, which wasn't much.

I curled onto my side, expecting to fight off that persistent chill. Instead, I purred as my fingers explored something hard, warm, and comforting.

Soft feathers met my touch as I explored outward. I sank my fingers into them, relishing the harsher edges of male wings that maintained heat so much better than my silky plumes.

But why are there male feathers here?

"Welcome back, sweet bird," a male voice said, making me go deathly still as arms wrapped around my middle and hoisted me closer to a naked, hard chest.

My eyes shot open, seeing Sorin's muscular back in front of me with my fingers tangled in his wings.

Oh, right. I'd been healing him.

Yet, we were on my mattress and Zian was at my back, trapping me between the two male bodies that I'd fantasized about for weeks.

"Uh, he's all healed now," I said as I futilely tried to untangle myself from my predicament. My wings were pressed into my back and impossible to extend with Zian so close to me. I pulled away from Sorin, only to find myself curling into Zian on the crowded mattress.

He nuzzled into my nape, not bothering to brush my hair aside as he inhaled. "Your scent is different when you heal," he murmured, the lilt to his voice slurring as if he was drugged. "It's stronger. No. It's pure." When his teeth tested my neck, I went still again and he chuckled. "Don't be afraid, sweet bird. I just want to thank you."

Thank me?

"You sure have some way of showing it," I said, my voice hopelessly husky with need.

I wasn't going to dare hope that Zian meant to relieve the sexual tension between us. He'd made it clear that any sort of physical advancement would only complicate things.

We were compatible, which meant we could permanently mate if our physical relationship progressed. If that happened, there was a multitude of torture the guards could use on us. Even something as simple as separation would destroy a newly mated pair.

But if we went on like this for much longer, I would be destroyed all the same.

His fingers drifted across my collarbone, the slight touch sending electricity zinging through my body as he ventured underneath my shirt. I was glad he couldn't see my mouth part on a silent gasp.

"I promise you'll enjoy it," he whispered with cruel intention underlining his words.

I whimpered when he plucked at the loop holding my top up. Cool air hit my breasts, and holy hell, there was no way I was going to be able to resist Zian if he wanted to take me right now.

The feminine sound escaping my mouth caused Sorin

to stir as if his body reacted to my need. He twisted, managing to fumble over his healed wings as he sat up on his forearm. He blinked a few times before grinning at us, his gaze dipping to take in the view. "Now I know I'm dreaming."

Zian stopped his slow torment to lean over me and press a kiss to Sorin's mouth. I watched, trapped between them as I tried to curl into myself. I'd seen them together, but I'd never been this up close and personal.

"I'm glad you're back," Zian said when they pulled away. "I worried—"

"Don't," Sorin said. He reached for Zian's chiseled shoulder as he added, "I'm here now."

A rare, genuine smile flashed across Zian's face. Not one of the smug grins he typically gave me, but a real joyous one that hinted at the Nora he had once been—what a Nora was meant to be.

Zian ran his fingers along the arch of one of Sorin's graceful wings. They truly were gorgeous, albeit massive, appendages that were taking up half the wall space. "Do they still hurt?" Zian asked.

Sorin flexed one of his wings over us, the movement breezing my hair from my face. "I've never felt this good, to be honest." His gaze fell to me as I squirmed and desperately tried to pull up my shirt, silently trying to escape them. "It seems we have this little dove to thank for my rejuvenated wings."

Zian looped his arm around me again, securing me once more between them as I squeaked in surprise. His deft touch sent the tattered fabric of my top to the ground, leaving my upper body exposed.

His chest warmed my back.

Sorin's body warmed my front.

This is so not going to end well.

My heart stopped when Sorin took my face in his hands, his thumbs running sweetly over my cheekbones. His eyes had often looked black from a distance, but now they glimmered deep blue like his tattoos, akin to sapphires in the night.

"You didn't have to heal me so thoroughly," he said, his voice low and gentle as he leaned in closer to me. "I can tell it weakened you."

He was right.

My stomach had a persistent ache that no amount of food could fix, and I knew my eyes would have that washed-out sheen they took on when I overextended myself. I managed to get by with sleep where I could grab it to restore my reserves when it got this bad, though I couldn't help but feel a sense of rejuvenation from Sorin's touch, so I leaned into it, my chest purring before I could think twice.

He went still, his mouth parting as his gaze fell to take in my body.

"Yeah, that's a thing she does now," Zian offered as he ran his fingers down Sorin's muscular chest, not stopping when he reached his waist. I realized with a blush that the angels were naked, and Sorin groaned as Zian wrapped his fingers around his growing erection.

Sorin leaned in and sucked my lower lip into his mouth before I understood what was happening. Salt and caramel exploded across my tongue, making me moan into his kiss, which only spurred him on. He threaded his fingers through my hair until he had a fistful at the roots, then he angled me to take his tongue as his hips moved against Zian's strokes.

I knew I should do something to stop this, but I was hopelessly entangled now. Salt and caramel and sin wrapped around me, making me forget all the possible ways this could go wrong.

Because it didn't *feel* wrong.

For the first time in my life, it felt like home.

I'd watched Zian and Sorin play together several times before Sorin's disappearance, and I didn't intend to close my eyes now that I was finally a part of their ecstasy. My eyelids fluttered open to find Sorin's hooded gaze watching me, his fingers still in my hair. "What do you want, little dove? I am not one to be in anyone's debt, so name your price."

I instantly knew what I wanted. My gaze fell to his beautiful cock, which Zian expertly stroked. My tongue flashed across my lips, rewarding me with a pained groan from Sorin. "Oh, dove, are you sure?"

My focus shifted upward once more, then I sought help from Zian. What I desired was something I had never done before. This was all so new, and I didn't want to fumble my way through it.

"I don't know how," I admitted, barely able to form the words as heat flushed over my chest.

Zian's midnight gaze drank in my taut nipples as he grinned. "Follow my lead, sweet bird. Just like this." He moved around me to kneel over Sorin, his irises capturing mine as he bent his head to taste Sorin's cock.

One swipe of his tongue had my thighs clenching.

A second lick had Sorin groaning.

And then Zian took every inch into his mouth in slow, measured movements, all while holding my gaze.

I swallowed hard.

Fuck, that's hot.

My arousal must have emitted more of my scent into the air, because Sorin bit back a growl as he grabbed Zian's mussed hair and forced him to take more. "Shit," Sorin breathed, his back bowing. "Keep doing that."

I swore Zian grinned, his expression knowing as he shifted his attention from me to Sorin and back to me again.

My chest heaved, my lungs constricting as I forgot how to breathe. They'd messed around before but never like this, not that I'd *seen*, anyway.

A whimper built inside, my thighs slick and ready for them despite my inexperience. I *wanted*. But I forced myself to focus on the demonstration, to watch Zian's head bob based on the cues Sorin gave him.

Shallow sucking when Sorin groaned or tried to take control of the motion.

Swallowing him to the hilt when Sorin released him, only to be grabbed once more.

"You're fucking killing me," Sorin accused on a harsh exhale. "Both of you."

Zian hummed in agreement, one of his palms slipping downward to fist himself while his opposite hand remained against Sorin's hip to hold him down.

My need mounted, their salted caramel scent taunting my instincts. I moved before I could stop myself, my lips tracing Zian's side, only to freeze as Sorin went stiff beneath us.

The male groaned loudly, his dick pulsing in Zian's mouth as he swallowed the other man's pleasure.

I want that, I thought, noting how Zian's hand still moved between his own legs. *Mine.*

It was such a natural concept, a declaration I felt come from deep within, and I shifted again on impulse alone.

Squeezing myself between them, I pushed aside Zian's hand and ran my tongue around the swollen edge of his cock before taking as much of his flesh into my mouth as I could.

Oh. Mmm.

I'd thought their scent was arousing, but this… *Fuck.* To taste Zian went beyond anything I could ever imagine.

Pure sex ran across my tongue with delicious sweetness, and I instantly lapped it up, licking and sucking and wanting more.

He shifted to allow me better access, his groan music to my ears.

"Shit, Sorin, make her stop that," Zian panted as he rolled to his back, his palm in my hair taking me with him.

Sorin chuckled as he shifted around on the bed, his weight dipping close to me. "Yeah, I don't think so, Z. She's clearly enjoying herself. But I have an idea that might help you out."

The devilish angel moved again, his heat nearing the ache between my thighs, but I couldn't see his intent or determine what he was up to. Stopping to look wasn't a choice. The heady rush of Zian's ecstasy was doing incredible things to me, building me into a frenzy that resulted in a gasp when a delicious spike of pleasure radiated from my left breast.

I paused, looking down to see Sorin's tongue flash out

84

and flick my nipple as he settled himself sideways on the bed beneath my torso. One of his hands disappeared between my legs, pushing aside the thin fabric covering my mound to swirl a circle over my clit.

What a puzzle we made on this small mattress.

Yet it was a conundrum I never wanted to leave.

Zian groaned as I released more of my arousal into the air. "That is *not* helping," he bit out.

Lost in a haze of need, I wrapped my lips around his cock again, cutting off whatever else he was about to say. I couldn't describe the feeling as rapture mounted in my core. I just knew I didn't want to scream, so I took Zian's cock as deep into my throat as I could.

Sorin's magic fingers worked over my folds in time with his tongue against my breast. His attentions danced across my nipple, sending electricity burning cold and hot all over my body. My hips angled, wanting any part of him inside of me that I could get, but he lightly bit down in punishment.

"Don't move, little dove," he chided, then peeled off what was left of my clothes as he kissed his way down and shifted around me to lie between my legs, forcing me to straddle his face.

Oh…

He sucked my clit, then licked me deep, repeating the motion in a harsh, commanding cycle that left me trembling above him.

I nearly released Zian, my focus spiraling to a foreign place of sensation. Only his delectable taste drew me back, reminding me of the prize I held within my mouth.

Sorin moved faster with agonizing circles until I thought I would die, one hand branding my hip to keep me in place as I tried to seek reprieve from the aching pleasure.

When a wave crested through my body, I squeezed Zian's shaft between my lips and salty caramel exploded into my throat, forcing me to pop off of him on a scream that demanded release.

Sorin chuckled, the vibration causing another quake to quiver through my limbs until I collapsed into a heap of feathers and male bodies, not caring if I ever woke again.

CHAPTER ELEVEN

ZIAN

PUSHING THE BUNKS TOGETHER was the best idea ever. It gave our wings room to sprawl out. We'd have to designate a new sparring space later, but for now, I was more than content to just lie here forever.

Except we had already been lounging here for quite a while.

Frowning, I glanced at the window, noting the dark sky.

The guards had allowed us to stay in our cell all day. Because they were enjoying the show on the camera? Or had they kept everyone in their respective areas?

Lifting to my elbows, I surveyed the room, searching for anything out of place. A tray of untouched food rested on the floor just inside the door, suggesting they'd opened it at some point without us hearing it.

A disconcerting thought.

One we needed to consider for later.

Unless... My brows came down. *Did they drug us?* That would explain how we slept through an entire day, perhaps more. Leaning over Raven, I pressed my mouth to Sorin's ear. "Wake up." I kept my tone soft, meaning to coax him to awareness without alarming him.

It worked.

His deep blue eyes opened slightly, one eyebrow arching. "You gonna suck me off again?"

I snorted. "One-track mind."

"Always."

"You're squishing me," Raven piped up, her delicious curves pressed to mine in a way I wanted to explore after we had this pertinent conversation.

I caught her hip with my palm before she could wiggle out from beneath me and lifted just enough to catch her gaze. "We missed at least a day."

"What?" They both spoke at the same time, but it was Sorin who glanced around the cell, his focus going to the window.

"Shit," he added, starting to sit up. "Is that normal?"

"No." This time it was my turn to speak at the same time as Raven. She really did fit well with us. And after our little oral prelude, I didn't mind the idea of keeping her. Smiling, I dipped to press my lips to hers, allowing myself only a few seconds of indulgence.

"Elaborate," Sorin said after clearing his throat.

"There's a schedule," I murmured, reluctantly rolling off Raven and onto my elbow beside her head. When she started to move, I slid my thigh over hers to hold her in place. We were absolutely going to play again after this discussion finished. "Most days start with breakfast. Then we go outside to stretch our wings, which usually ends badly for at least one Noir. There's typically a challenge exercise every seven days—"

"Except for the one we just did. That was only four days after the last one," Raven put in.

I nodded. "Right, it came early. But there was an influx of newcomers this week, more so than usual. They've been arriving daily in packs of five to seven. About twenty came in the other day after the last cull, with twenty more the next day."

"So we probably should have expected an acceleration on the challenge." Raven scrunched her nose. "But we've never had a day in the cell like this."

"And I suspect they drugged us," I muttered, looking pointedly at the tray. "Because there's no way I would have missed someone opening that door, nor have we ever gotten free handouts when it comes to food."

"We've also been alternating night shifts, too," Raven murmured. "But we all slept this time."

"Why are you alternating shifts?" Sorin asked.

"Night terrors." I cringed. We weren't actually sure what to call them, but the term seemed adequate enough. "They started with Mister Slobbers, as Raven lovingly nicknamed him."

"Mister Slobs," she corrected, which I knew she would. "It seemed more appropriate than Mister Almost Killed Z."

Sorin's eyebrows shot up. "Something almost killed you?"

"Apparently," I grumbled, still sour over the incident. "He wielded an enchanted dagger that would have made me bleed out if Raven hadn't worked her magic."

Her lips twitched. "Turns out I'm useful after all."

I leaned over her again, my palm settling over her tit and giving it a squeeze. "Very useful." She opened her mouth to protest, but I silenced her with a kiss that involved a good amount of tongue. My dick hardened against her thigh, eager for another round with her mouth. Or maybe something else warm and wet.

Her fingers wove through my hair, tightening with interest, only to lock in place as a familiar hiss entered the cell.

Speaking of the night terrors...

I acted on instinct, flying out of the bunk—literally—to get some height on the bastard forming in the corner. We'd determined after four nights together that they always arrived in the same spot, opposite the door and near the window.

This guy drooled just like the others, his sulfuric stench causing me to gag.

Raven joined me, her affinity for talking to creatures coming in handy as she addressed the monster. "You have two options. Leave or we kill you."

The thing snarled, making a translation unnecessary.

But Raven told me his thoughts anyway. "He's opted for option number two."

"I figured."

We circled the thing, our hands free and ready.

I mentally counted down from five, the slobbery abomination producing his weapon on my second count. Raven acted, her steps sure as she went in low to grab the thing's wrist, giving it a twist to knock the enchanted item free. I plucked it off the ground in a practiced move and sent it sailing into the thing's chest cavity.

It screamed.

I smiled.

It died.

Raven high-fived me when the thing dissipated into the usual puddle, slithering down the corner drain. "Eleven seconds this time," she said.

"Not bad," I replied. "Going to break ten tomorrow?"

"Sure."

I wrapped my arm around her, tugging her into my side, and turned us both to face a slack-jawed Sorin. "What's up, bro? You look like you've seen a night terror. Oh, wait…"

Raven giggled, the sound a comfort in the otherwise dark environment.

"What the hell just happened?" Sorin demanded.

"Night terror," I repeated, hooking a thumb over my shoulder. "They show up in the corner around two or three in the morning every single night."

"So far," Raven said.

"Yeah. So far." It could change at any given second, and likely would.

This place had become predictable, and something told me that wasn't the point at all. They wanted to keep us on our toes, almost as if they were trying to weed out all the weaklings in favor of the stronger Noir. What I couldn't figure out was why or what purpose they had behind it, other than to create a strong reformatory of violent criminals.

"This place is literal hell." A haunted gleam entered Sorin's expression, one I'd noticed lurking in his gaze when he'd arrived at the gym yesterday, or whenever that was. Whatever happened during his captivity these last couple of weeks, it hadn't been good.

I'd ask him about it eventually, as I knew better than to press now. Sometimes horrors were better left buried. Given the state his wings had been in when he returned, I could very easily assume that his experience had definitely been one of those horrors.

Which meant he needed a distraction.

Perhaps in the form of a pretty little Raven.

"Hell, yes," I agreed with him. "But the view is spectacular." I punctuated my point by allowing my gaze to roam freely over Raven's gloriously naked body. All of us were in the nude, not having bothered to put anything on after our intimate introduction. A good thing, truly, because covering Raven's beautiful form would be a sin.

Her skin flushed beneath my open perusal, her tongue sneaking out to dampen her lips. I loved that she didn't try to cover herself, granting me full access to my appreciation.

Which she returned in kind by stroking her attention over my body and Sorin's with sweet desire. My cock saluted her, causing her lips to twitch. "You two are insatiable," she whispered. "Have you always fucked each other every day? Or was that for my benefit?"

I cocked a brow. "Fucked each other?" We had yet to do that in her presence, preferring our hands either on each other or on ourselves while we taunted her with our scents. It seemed only fair considering her citrusy aroma surrounded us day and night.

"Yeah. Well, you know."

"No, actually. I don't think I do," Sorin murmured, taking a predatory step forward to draw his fingertips up her side in a proprietary motion. It confirmed his instincts rivaled mine, his need to claim the ideal mate riding him hard despite our short acquaintance. After a century without a female's touch, it made sense. That Raven happened to be compatible only worsened our craving.

I joined him on her other side, mimicking his motions but along her opposite rib cage. "Define *fucking*, sweet bird."

"Wh-what?"

"You heard me," I whispered, leaning in to nibble her earlobe. "Define what *fucking* means to you."

"What you two were doing before Sorin disappeared?" She phrased it as a suggestion, her voice hitching at the end.

"That wasn't fucking," Sorin said, kissing her neck and closing the gap between his body and hers.

"Maybe we should show her how it's done." I copied his actions, drawing my lips down her throat to her collarbone and meeting his gaze. "You good?"

He knew what I meant and nodded to accept my offer. My already hard dick throbbed in anticipation. We rarely went this far with each other, mostly because neither of us enjoyed submitting. But for her, he was willing to provide a demonstration. It likely helped that I'd been the one to suck him off during our last session.

Sorin threaded his fingers through Raven's dark hair and pulled her in for a long, sensuous kiss. She practically melted against him, her body eager to play. All these weeks cooped up in a cell with two virile males had clearly impacted her as well, her orange-like scent permeating the air in an intoxicating wave.

I bit her neck, loving the way her pulse skyrocketed beneath my tongue, and licked a dangerous path down to her glorious tits. Her nipples beaded in welcome, her feminine form primed and ready for sex.

Yet her virginity held me back.

At least for now.

I wanted her to be absolutely sure before we crossed that line because there would be no coming back. Once I seated my cock inside her, I'd have no choice but to finalize the claim. We were too compatible for me to resist, my urge to mate her stronger than ever before.

Warrior Nora didn't take partners.

It went against our code.

We were born to protect. That didn't mean we couldn't fuck; we just weren't supposed to claim.

Noir had no such rules.

If I wanted to take her, I could. However, I required her permission and understanding first.

So I'd play with Sorin instead, give her a show, and enjoy her reaction in kind.

Taking her stiff peak between my lips, I gave her a gentle nibble before sucking hard enough to draw a moan from her throat. Sorin swallowed it, his tongue still laving hers, teaching her how to indulge his preferences. He preferred harsh movements and dominant sweeps, while I tended to take my time, kissing thoroughly and possessing every inch of a woman's mouth.

Sorin and I frequently battled when we locked lips, his need occasionally overpowering mine and vice versa. Always a new experience, always arousing. However, Raven offered a new opportunity with her soft curves and submissive qualities. A fighter lurked beneath her skin, but on the surface, she caved to our touch. And I adored her all the more for it.

I slid to my knees, my mouth traveling down her flat abdomen to the curls between her thighs. She jolted as I nipped her clit, her pussy already wet and eager for my attention. I gave in to the desire to suck her sensitive little nub into my mouth, having allowed Sorin the first taste earlier.

It was my turn to know her intimately, to drown myself in her scent. She didn't disappoint, her hips shifting forward in delicious little movements that encouraged me to tongue her thoroughly and completely.

I loved that she didn't shy away from my face between her thighs, that she rode my mouth without shame. Sorin palmed her breast, giving it a squeeze and drawing another of those sexy moans from her.

Sliding two fingers inside her tight heat, I flexed them, learning her reactions with each stroke. Deeper penetration made her inner walls squeeze, shallow touches caused her to groan in frustration, and rhythmic thrusts caused goose bumps to pebble up and down her thighs.

She appeared ready to fall, her knees wobbling as her pleasure mounted.

Sorin sensed it, his body shifting behind her as one arm wrapped around her waist to hold her upright, his opposite palm still playing with her tits. She angled her face backward to continue kissing him, giving me an exquisite view of their embrace as I watched from between her thighs.

Her pants grew heavier, causing her breasts to sway. A gorgeous red pattern danced along her skin, confirming what my fingers and tongue already knew—she was close.

Sorin bit down on her lower lip, his nose brushing hers. "Are you going to come for us, little dove?" he asked, his tone deep with arousal.

"Yes," she breathed, writhing against my mouth. "Yes…"

I bit back a smile at the hiss in her voice and instead slid my teeth against her flesh, guessing that she needed a little bit *more* to shove her over the edge.

I was right.

She threw her head back on a gasp, her body falling apart beneath our touch in a glorious display of pure sex. *Fuck*, I wanted to slide into her throbbing cunt while Sorin took her from behind.

Not yet, I told myself.

She didn't even know what fucking was—at least, if her earlier comments were to be believed. So we would teach her. Show her how we liked it. And then see if she wanted to proceed.

Her lips parted on a sigh, her legs seeming to give out beneath her. Sorin held her steady, his lips curling in amusement. "I foresee a game in our future," he said, his gaze finding mine as I released her pleasured nub from my lips. "We'll have to see who can make her scream the loudest. So far, I'm winning."

I narrowed my gaze. "Careful or I'll make you scream the loudest."

Heat glimmered in his ocean depths. "I don't scream."

True. He growled or snarled depending on his mood.

Sorin stepped back to help lower Raven to the bed, propping her up on the pillows and spreading her legs wide. *Mmm, yes.* I approved of his intentions, my excitement mounting as he went to kneel between her thighs.

Raven gazed up at us through hooded eyes, her cheeks pink. "What now?"

"Now?" I gave her a grin that would probably be described as feral. "Now we're going to fuck."

Chapter Twelve

SORIN

RAVEN'S LIPS PARTED, a hint of unease entering her gaze.

I knew what Zian meant, but she'd interpreted it differently.

Leaning down, I took her mouth in another sweet kiss while Zian joined us on the bed, his hand slipping between her thighs once more. She trembled, her heart beating wildly in her chest.

I kissed a path to her ear while Zian repositioned himself behind me, his fingers questing across my rump to the place he intended to penetrate. Using her natural lubricant, he parted my cheeks and began the process of readying me to accept him.

"Don't worry, little dove," I whispered to her, my tongue tracing the shell of her ear. "Zian is going to fuck me, not you."

She frowned, her brow furrowing. "What do you

mean?"

Ah, her sweet innocence pricked at my heart, confirming our need to ease her into our shared intimacy all the more. "He's going to fuck my ass," I told her bluntly. "And it's going to make me come all over your pussy."

"Then he's going to massage it into your clit and make you come again," Zian added, his fingers pumping in and out of me in a much harsher movement than what he'd done between her legs. Mostly because he knew I could take it and he got off on that knowledge.

Poor Raven wouldn't know what to do with herself the first time Zian fucked her.

It wouldn't be soft or coaxing, but hard and demanding.

My shaft pulsed at the notion, the image of their intimacy making me hard as fuck. I loved watching Zian, and it'd been so long since I'd seen him take a female. Just as long as it'd been since I had one beneath me.

Oh, I hoped Raven could handle us.

Because if not, it was going to be a rough future in this cell. Assuming we all survived this nightmare. I shuddered as I thought of Brina and her scalpel, having no desire to ever see that wicked bitch ever again.

Zian shoved another digit inside me, the pressure snapping me back to his movements and to the gorgeous female sprawled out beneath me on the bed. He bit my shoulder, the sharp pinch a silent reprimand for falling out of the moment.

He hadn't asked about what happened and wouldn't until I brought it up, but he knew. He always knew.

Another bite confirmed it, his dominance showing as he forced me to remain alert and aware during our shared experience. He wanted my focus.

I nearly thanked him for the distraction from my thoughts.

But he added a fourth finger and I cursed instead, the pressure too much.

He didn't stop, the sadist in him enjoying my reaction far too much to give me even a second to acclimate. I was surprised he didn't just take me as he usually did, then realized he was easing us all into it for Raven's benefit.

And maybe a little bit for mine.

He knew I'd suffered, and didn't want to add to it. Yet I'd welcome his brand of agony over Brina's any day.

"Just do it," I told him, my voice hoarse. "I can take it."

"Oh, I know you can," he replied, his tongue laving the wound he'd left on my shoulder. Because, yeah, the bastard had made me bleed.

"Dick," I muttered.

He chuckled, the sound husky and filled with sensual promise. Raven quivered beneath me, her pussy flooding with renewed desire. It took restraint not to bend down and lick her clean. Instead, I fisted my cock while she watched, my wings helping me to balance on my knees over her. The intense throbbing in my balls told me I wouldn't last long, that I'd spill my seed all over her pretty cunt in minutes after Zian took control.

We should probably do this more often, except neither of us enjoyed the inferior position. However, the sensation of his cock pulsating against my prostate certainly created an explosion unlike any other. Oh, but I bet Raven's tight little hole could create competition for the best orgasm. As if she knew the direction of my thoughts, a fresh aromatic wave of oranges touched my senses, causing me to tighten my grip.

"Fuck," I breathed, my lower abdomen tightening from that single stroke. "You'd better take me while you can, Z."

"I can take you whenever I want," he returned, the dark words a whisper against my ear and creating a trail of goose bumps down my neck.

"Only when I offer it," I countered.

He removed his fingers and gripped my hip with his opposite hand. "Yeah?" The head of his cock lined up with the tight ring of my ass, deepening the anticipation. "I think you like me inside you, Sorin." He thrust forward, eliciting a growl from my throat as my entire body went up in flames from the intrusion. "And that sound proves it."

A curse fell from my lips as I nearly fell forward, but my feathers kept me steady, allowing me to take his punishing strokes while he worked himself into the position he desired.

Raven's little gasp drew my gaze downward to find two lust-blown pupils staring up at me. Her cheeks had gone from pink to red, her lips parted on a pant as she watched Zian bottom out inside me.

This was fucking. Not the hand shit. And now she knew. I could see the realization forming in her expression and could smell it in her scent.

Who knew oranges could be so damn arousing?

I held her gaze while Zian pumped into me, allowed her to see the ecstasy he inspired with each savage thrust.

Because damn, he knew how to fucking move. He didn't go easy on me, not that I'd expected him to. Had he tried, I would have called him on it. A bad session with Doctor Insane Bitch didn't equate to weakness. Besides, Raven had healed me to the point where I felt brand new.

"Shit, Z," I grunted out after a particularly harsh thrust.

"You're drifting," he accused, always fucking aware of my mental state. "When I'm inside you, I expect your undivided attention." He slammed into me even harder, literally driving his point home. It caused my wings to flare outward to help me remain balanced on my knees.

My grip automatically tightened, my opposite hand fisting.

Part of me wanted to fight back, to retaliate, but Raven's intense expression captivated me and drew me back to the moment. She looked ready to explode again, her breasts flushed prettily and begging for attention.

And that gorgeous pussy.

Fuck, it was so damn wet. It'd be so easy to lie over her, thrust deep, and sandwich myself between her and Zian.

My groin tensed, my orgasm mounting by the second. I wanted to spill myself all over her, demand she rub my essence deep into her skin, and make her come from my heat alone.

We already told her that was the plan.

Now it was time to make that plan a reality.

"I'm close," I said, my muscles tensing as an inferno

blazed in my lower abdomen. "Fuck, it's going to be big, too." I could feel it twisting angrily, threatening to explode against my will. But I held it back, wanting to prolong the moment, to give Zian time to catch up to me.

And catch up to me, he did, his pace quickening into a violent dance between our hips.

I finally gave in to the desire to fall forward, catching myself on one palm beside Raven's head as I continued to pump my shaft with my opposite hand.

"I'm going to come all over you, baby," I warned her. "Then you're going to help me massage it into your skin, into your cunt, all over that sweet little nub, until you come again on a scream so intense you'll forget how to breathe."

She visibly shuddered, her breath fanning over my face and tickling the loose strands of white hair that had fallen around her in a curtain of false privacy.

"Now," Zian demanded, his fingers digging into my hip as he angled me backward to accept his fierce movements.

A low groan worked its way up my throat, parting my lips, as a sensual fire caressed my veins, the warmth building, churning, *consuming* my existence until stars went off behind my eyes. I shook beneath the onslaught, oblivion stealing my ability to think or move as I bathed Raven's sweet heat in my cum.

Rope after rope after rope of my essence coated her folds, her curls, her lower belly, and her thighs. And fuck if the arousing scene didn't make me want to come all over again.

"Put your hand between your thighs, sweet bird," Zian demanded, his violent hold on my hip telling me he wasn't far behind in his own pleasure. "I want to see you pleasure yourself with Sorin's cum."

She moaned, her pupils so wide I could no longer see her irises.

"Now, Raven," I told her, my voice hoarse. "Do it now."

Her whimper made me smile. It was such a needy, aroused sound. I loved knowing we'd brought her to this point, that our words and actions were driving her mad enough with yearning that she did exactly what we wanted without question.

She slipped a finger through her wetness, my pleasure mingling with her own as she dutifully rubbed the two essences together.

"Help her," Zian said. "Fucking help her."

I released my cock to press my thumb to her clit, causing her to bow off the bed.

A few circles of her sweet little bud sent her cascading over the edge just as Zian found his climax inside me, his growl nearing a snarl as he bit my shoulder to keep himself quiet. It flattened my wings, his chest crushing me as I balanced us both on one palm, my other hand busy helping Raven draw out her orgasm. She'd slipped two fingers inside her tight sheath, which made my cock jump in approval.

Because those fingers had been coated in my essence.

And now I was inside her.

That thought alone almost made me come again, but I focused on her instead. Rubbing her intently, ensuring my seed touched every intimate part of her. I massaged it into her thighs, her lower belly, her curls, her pussy lips, and again into her clit. Until she wiggled in protest, her sensitized skin unable to take any more.

So I leaned down to kiss her while Zian cleaned up behind me.

The water ran momentarily, his shower brief, and then he joined us with a set of washcloths. I used one on myself, then considered Raven. "Do you want me to clean you up?" I asked her. "Or do you want to sleep while coated in my essence?" Some females liked that, mostly because of the mating scents.

Raven yawned and snuggled into me, providing her answer. Zian smiled as he drew her back into his abdomen, his lips caressing her neck in a sweet kiss before he met my gaze. "You good?"

It was the same question as before when he asked for permission to fuck me.

"I'm good," I confirmed.

He nodded once, his dark eyes holding a wealth of gratitude that he'd never admit out loud, before closing them to sleep.

I draped my wing around them both, Raven's head pressed to my chest, and joined them in momentary bliss.

Only to be awoken far too soon by an odd squeaking sound.

Raven stirred, lifting her head. "What is it, Mousey Mouse?"

"You still have your pet?" I asked, surprised Zian hadn't tried to eat the thing by now. Mice weren't our favorite, but protein was protein.

She ignored me, her focus on the squeaking. "I see," she murmured. "Thank you for letting us know."

The mouse disappeared, causing me to frown. "What did it say?"

"That the demon creatures in solitary with Novak keep trying to engage him, but he isn't talking to anyone," she murmured, yawning. "Yet he seems fine otherwise."

"Novak?" I repeated, confused. "You know where he is?"

"Yeah, in some sort of solitary wing," she said, her eyes falling closed. "The prison has a lot of sections."

"It's a massive maze of different units for various paranormal beings," Zian added, his voice soft with sleep. "*Nightmare Penitentiary* is what the mouse calls it. Novak's stuck in solitary with four insane demons who are obsessed with some female, but the mouse says Novak's fine. Which matches what I feel."

"Can we get him out?" I asked, already pretty sure of the answer, given my experience with Brina.

"Mouse says it's impossible and we need to wait for him to come back. Said the same about you." Zian joined the yawning game, then nuzzled the back of Raven's neck. "We should sleep. The schedule is shifting again, so we need to be prepared."

"Who should keep guard?" Raven asked groggily, her pleasured body already well on its way to dreamland.

"Keep guard?" I repeated.

102

"Night terrors," Zian muttered.

"Right. I'll stay up." Because I wasn't tired at all, my mind whirring with memories of the portals and all the supernatural hoops I'd gone through to reach Brina and then return.

This place was a fucking maze.

And Noir Reformatory itself was a death trap.

When Novak, Z, and I first fell into the reformatory system, we hadn't tried to escape out of loyalty to our warrior roots. We believed that if we repented enough, we'd earn back our white feathers.

That never happened.

So we embraced our fates and used our skills to achieve a high-level status in our former prison, mostly to survive.

Noir Reformatory required a new strategy, one based on escape and not just survival.

"Wake me when you want a nap." That came from Zian.

I never woke him, my mind refusing to sleep.

CHAPTER THIRTEEN

RAVEN

ANOTHER WEEK, ANOTHER CULLING.

My nerves no longer reacted to culling day because things had changed. Noir Reformatory had morphed into something more bearable now that I had given in to playing with my sexy-as-sin Noir cellmates.

I thought I'd known what it meant to mate, but after I witnessed what Zian did to Sorin, I realized there was so much they intended to teach me.

And they were taking their time.

Mesmerized, I watched Zian add another fluid design to Sorin's tattoo along his right arm. I had a feeling it was painful, given the blood that dripped from his wrist, but a smirk lit his face, amused by my interest.

At one point during Sorin's absence, Zian had acquired the tools he needed for tattooing. I suspected it was a result of his *heart-eater* nickname. No one wanted to argue with him over anything, fearful he'd call on them in the ring next.

The two males had spent most of the week touching up the marks on Sorin's tats, each one resembling a tribute to someone he'd killed—of which there'd been many at Noir Reformatory, even with his absence.

I sat cross-legged on the floor, much closer this time, intrigued by the pattern weaving energy across Sorin's skin.

"What kind of magic is that?" I asked, taking note of how Zian elegantly carved the art with blue magic over Sorin's skin with his fingertips. He created the blue ink with whatever items he'd acquired, but he applied it through his hands using some sort of foreign power. It reminded me of my healing magic, but one that burned and branded, leaving the permanent layer of skin scarred.

It intrigued me that pain could be turned into something so beautiful.

Sorin had explained that each mark represented a life he'd taken. The ink running up the entirety of his left arm and the biceps of his right suggested he'd taken a lot of lives.

Today's life had belonged to his opponent in the ring.

Zian flicked his wrist, sending his blue magic puffing into a tiny flame to seal the design, then he leaned down and licked the wound clean. It was a primal move, as well as an intimate one. We all had been indulging our animalistic instincts lately. I hadn't yet decided if that made us stronger or if it would come back to bite us in the ass when we were inevitably separated, or worse.

"It's repentance magic," Sorin answered, referring to the question I'd asked Zian regarding the power he used for the tats.

Meeting and holding my gaze, he added, "Before Zian's Fall, his energy was used as a punishment. He could make Nora forget in an effort to set them on the right track, with the markings serving as a warning of how close they came to Falling. It plays tricks on the mind not to know what you did wrong and sort of scares you into perfection."

Zian snorted but didn't comment.

"It doesn't work the way it used to as a result of his Fall," Sorin continued. "But I'm good with it because I don't want to lose my memories."

Zian smirked. "It's kind of a fuck-you to the Nora that we use it to create tattoos."

Sorin nodded. "Yeah, with them, I'll never forget what they've made me become."

I made a face, which earned me a knowing look from Zian as he finished the tattoo.

"I know. It's technically a Nora trait, but we were all Nora once, sweet bird." He kissed my forehead and tucked a strand of hair behind my ear. "Well, most of us, anyway."

Sorin raised a brow. "What's that's supposed to mean?"

Zian ran tender kisses down my throat, his lingering magic making his lips hot against my skin. I couldn't imagine Zian with white wings or see him forcing anyone to forget their sins. That kind of brainwashing was one of the many reasons I detested the Nora and was glad to have never been born among them.

"She claims that she was born as this exquisite creature," Zian said, tracing my lower lip with the fingers he'd played across Sorin's skin. "Mmm, you make me want to Fall all over again, sweet bird."

His teeth went to my neck, changing from hot kisses to punishing nips. My breath quickened, knowing Zian's appetite always started this way and soon I'd be entangled with the two of them, at their mercy as they taught me new and delicious things.

Sorin watched me, his gaze smoldering, but he let Zian play as he traced over the new tattooed mark with a single finger. He didn't seem regretful over his actions, merely respectful.

Sorin was a killer.

As were we all.

A bang at our cell door made us all jump up, taking note of an amused Nora guard. I had no doubt the sickos watched us and got off on it. Lately they'd allowed us entire days alone in our cell to indulge our needs, even providing meals to keep up our strength.

I didn't like to dwell on why.

"Everyone to the yard," the guard barked, yanking the

door open and walking off. It wasn't like there was anywhere to go with the corridors leading only to the breakfast lounge, the yard, and the gym.

Sorin was on his feet in an instant, pulling up some pants—because, yeah, the guys rarely bothered with pants around me anymore—and squeezed his massive wings to his back to make it through the doorway. "Stay close, little dove."

I ducked my head and fell into step behind him with Zian at my back. We'd just had a culling this morning, so I was at a loss as to what the guards had in store for us now. The only thing I could think of was the rumors Zian had heard for a while now that a change was coming, something big enough to disrupt our tentative hierarchy. With the number of kills we were accruing, the inmates didn't have the numbers or alliances to take us on.

And oh, they wanted a taste of me.

It was another reason I was enjoying the small reprieve of being locked up in our cell together for long stretches at a time. Whether I was ready to admit it or not, I belonged to Sorin and Zian now, or I would soon anyway, once they took a more final, permanent step in our mating.

I wanted them both.

I craved them both.

If anyone wanted to fuck with us, they were going to have a hell of a fight on their hands.

The inmates paired off into groups and eyed a new collection of recruits at the end of the yard. I nearly slammed into Sorin's back when he abruptly came to a halt.

"Sorin," I complained, fussing with his feathers that had gotten in my mouth. "Don't just—"

"We need to get back to the cell immediately," Sorin snapped, shoving out a hand to keep me behind him so that I couldn't see a thing.

Zian peeked around his shoulder and spat out a curse.

"What is it?" I snapped, my feathers bristling with irritation. The two males wedged me between them with a spike of protectiveness that had me both annoyed and worried.

107

"Get her back to the cell," Sorin ordered, but I wasn't going to deal with his alpha bullshit. When he tried to swipe at me again, I bit down hard on his hand, making him flinch away with a curse.

Dipping under his arm, I sped around him and flapped my wings to get some distance.

Then I saw what had him so worried.

"Oh, shit," I said under my breath.

Valkyries.

It might not be apparent to the Nora, but I recognized this breed of females immediately. Their features had harder edges to them, even their feathers having subtle spotting in the primaries, but what really gave them away was their scent. It rubbed me the wrong way immediately and set my instincts on fire.

The three warrior females spotted me instantly, their heads jerking to lock onto me as their lips lifted in a snarl and their nostrils flared.

This was not good.

I heard Zian shouting something behind me, but my territorial instincts took over, shooting me toward the new females. Because no matter what kind of hellhole I was in, this was my place. Zian and Sorin were going to be my mates, and these bitches weren't going to take them.

It was an irrational line of thought, and perhaps this was where indulging my primal side for too long was coming back to bite me in the ass, but if there was one thing I'd learned about prison, it was to establish boundaries with new recruits immediately.

"There's a breeder here," said one with a snarl. "How'd she survive this long?"

Another of the females wrapped a long leg around a male she'd decided to toy with. The moron thought he was in heaven when she was probably just going to chop his balls off later.

"Who cares?" she said, running a finger under the male's chin. "She probably found some protectors. She won't last long once they're done with her. We've got bigger birds to burn anyway." She grinned, her sharpened teeth making me want to shrink into my wings.

A sudden urge to flee came on just as quickly as my territorial instincts from seconds ago.

"Hmm," said the third one with hair almost as dark as mine as she squinted. "There they are." She grinned as Zian grabbed my arm. "Keep your pet out of our way, will you? We're not looking for mates, so she can calm the fuck down."

"I'm right here," I snapped.

Sorin took his time appraising the three females, and they likewise took their time checking him out, raking their gazes over him until my blood boiled.

"Well, hello there," said the one with the long legs, discarding the male she'd been playing with to run her fingers over Sorin's muscular shoulder.

Mine.

The primal rage inside of me was quieted when Zian whispered in my ear. "You're making a scene, sweet bird." He cleared his throat and raised his voice. "She gets away from us sometimes, but that keeps it interesting."

I knew he was just putting on a show for the Valkyries to make me less of a target, but it still twisted my heart.

"Well, make sure it doesn't happen again," snapped the dark-haired one as her green eyes glared at me. "I eat breeders for lunch."

A fight broke out nearby as a Noir landed a hard punch on his neighbor. It became clear that with three more females added to the block, and weeks of having me out of their reach, the males were about to lose their shit.

The Valkyries watched the males fight over them, clearly amused to see who was going to come out on top. Meanwhile, I scanned the towers, wondering what the Nora were up to now. Because I could feel them watching me, waiting for a reaction.

They'd placed these three Valkyries here deliberately and then called us to the yard to let our introductions play out.

Bastards.

I accepted Sorin's hand that tugged me back to our cell,

but I couldn't shake my instincts that wanted to maim the three new females until they were nothing but feathers and pulp.

The fact that Zian and Sorin hadn't put them in their place said they saw the Valkyries as formidable enemies.

I didn't give a shit. If they were going to come at me, let them try. I'd faced worse.

I think.

CHAPTER FOURTEEN

SORIN

A Few Days Later...

"I DON'T LIKE THE WAY they're looking at her," I muttered to Zian as he finished another round of pull-ups in the makeshift gym.

He dropped to his feet and wiped the sweat from his brow before folding his arms over his bare chest. "Neither do I."

The three Valkyries stood off to the side watching Raven while she performed another round of bodyweight exercises on the mat. If she was aware of their scrutiny, she didn't show it, her focus on completing the set Zian had instructed her to do. "At least she's getting stronger."

"And more fluid in her steps," Zian agreed. "But those females have at least thirty years of experience on her. Except for the middle one. She's closer to Raven's age."

"Yeah, I noticed that. I think those other two are her

mentors." Similar to what Zian and I were doing for Raven.

Some females went the warrior route when they refused to mate. The more powerful they were, the harder it was to be taken over by a male-driven society. They also banded together in colonies, giving them strength in numbers.

Only idiots tried to fuck them. Valkyries were notorious for taking lovers to suit their needs, then killing them afterward. It was why they tended to go for warriors, preferring a challenge both in the bed and outside of it.

Hence their noticeable interest in me and Zian.

Not a chance in hell would we agree to play. Oh, we'd indulged a few Valkyries in the past, mostly because they were animals in the sack and could handle more than the average Nora female. But the after-party sucked.

Zian and I watched as yet another imbecile tried his luck.

And failed.

Because only the worthiest of males would be chosen by a Valkyrie for mating.

I smirked. "They'll never learn."

"They're desperate," Zian replied. "Desperation often leads to stupidity."

"Too true." The Valkyries began to train again, but their focus continued to return to Raven. When they first arrived, I thought they might try to recruit her to strengthen their numbers. But they had disliked Raven from the beginning, calling her a *breed*—

A fist met my abdomen, the impact coming from a very pissed-off little dove. "You could at least give me a chance to prove my worth before considering an upgrade," she snapped, her voice low and meant for us alone.

I shared a bewildered look with Zian before meeting her livid gaze. "What the hell are you talking about?"

"You're openly ogling the fresh meat like I'm not even here," she growled, the sound adorably ferocious. It made me want to pin her to the mattress and make her repeat it with my cock deep inside her. "You haven't even tried to properly fuck me yet. Maybe I'll surprise you. Who knows? But you won't if you keep checking out the replacement crop."

Zian's eyebrows shot upward. "Checking out the replacement crop?"

My lips twitched. "Someone's feeling possessive."

"How could I possibly feel possessive?" she countered, fire dancing in her expression. "You're not really mine, right? Just compatible and messing around. Nothing more." She turned on her heels to stomp away, but I caught her hip to yank her wings into my chest.

Zian stepped in front of her, blocking her path for good measure. "Nothing more?" A note of incredulity touched his tone. "I really hope you don't mean that."

"You're the one over here eye-banging a bunch of Valkyries instead of fucking me," she returned, sounding like a petulant little brat who needed a reminder of her place between us.

I bit her neck, right over her thundering pulse. "I don't like the accusation in your tone, little dove."

"It's not an accusation," she seethed, drawing attention from the room.

Zian met my gaze, communicating our next steps without words.

We couldn't have this conversation here, not within earshot of the Valkyries and the abundance of intrigued males.

"Back to the cell," Zian said, the command meant for Raven.

"No. I'm not done with my set."

"It wasn't a request," I whispered, my lips brushing her ear. "Get back to the cell now, little dove, or I'll carry you myself."

She bristled, her feathers tensing. "You can't just own me one minute and replace me the next."

"Actually, we can," Zian corrected her. "We're not mates, as you pointed out."

"Because you won't fuck me," she retorted, her voice rising above the seething murmur of moments ago and drawing far too many gazes our way.

"That's about to change," I told her quietly, shoving her

forward into Zian's waiting hands. He wrapped a possessive arm around her lower back to guide her out of the room and down the hall.

Now she remained quiet.

Now she obeyed.

Only because of the promise underlining my words.

I shook my head, amused. "If you wanted to be fucked so badly, little dove, all you needed to do was ask," I said as we returned to our cell and shut the door. It didn't lock since this was technically our free time, but our Raven required a different form of physical training today.

She sputtered as she spun around to face me. "That's not what this is about."

I backed her into the metal pole of our joint bunk beds, my brow inching upward in challenge. "That's exactly what this is about. Now strip before I rip the clothes off you."

"Sorin—"

"Now, Raven," Zian interjected, yanking her away from the pole so he could position himself behind her.

She swallowed, her citrusy scent blossoming around us in yearning and excitement, while a twinge of fear dilated her pupils. "I d-didn't mean—"

I grabbed her halter top and tore it from her torso, revealing her pert tits and her beautifully erect nipples. She yelped in response, her fingers quickly working on the button of her jeans.

"We should tan your hide for that display," Zian muttered, his lips finding her exposed shoulder as he helped her tug the fabric from her hips. "You practically demanded us to fuck you in a room full of spectators."

"No, I—"

"Yes," I corrected her, not wanting to hear whatever excuse she tried to issue. "Your possessive instincts are taking over because you haven't been properly claimed, and you blame us for that. So we'll fix it."

"Sounds like a good solution to me." Zian nibbled a path along her spine between her feathers as he knelt to remove the jeans from her legs.

She shivered but didn't object.

114

Because this had been the point of her little outburst.

Sure, the presence of the Valkyries had escalated her reaction. However, it was the underlying need in Raven's soul that exacerbated her actions.

Zian met my gaze again as he stood up behind her, our beautiful Raven deliciously naked between us. We'd already agreed that I'd be the one to take her first, my proclivities in the bedroom not as harsh as his. And while she might think we were angry at her right now, we really weren't. Her desire to fuck rivaled our own, the need to stake our connection riding all three of us in equal measure.

"Are you wet, sweet bird?" Zian asked, his hand reaching around to dip between her thighs. She swallowed, her cheeks darkening to the pink shade I favored on her. The flush crept downward to her chest, tightening her little points that much more.

I bent to take a stiff peak into my mouth, drawing a moan from her throat as Zian simultaneously slid his fingers inside her.

"Oh, she's ready," he murmured, approval radiating from his tone. "No wonder she caused such a scene. She's dripping for us, Sorin."

"Mmm," I hummed against her skin, my tongue circling her taut flesh before switching to her other breast. She threaded her fingers through my hair, her body giving us welcoming cues while her mouth stayed silent. "Do you want us to fuck you, Raven? To claim you properly?"

"Or are you hoping we'll replace you with a Valkyrie?" Zian taunted, his tone holding a touch of cruelty.

It reignited the fire in her, causing her to thrash between us, her head whipping around to flash a glower his way. "Don't you dare."

He smiled. "Then tell us to fuck you, sweet bird. Tell us to take you. To complete you. Because we both know that's really what this is about, baby. You want us inside you."

"Admit it and we'll give you everything you want and more." I drew my teeth down her sternum to her flat belly and lower to her sweet curls. "Unless all you want is my tongue." Zian removed his fingers, allowing me to lick her deep from her slick channel up to her pulsing nub. She shuddered, her grip in my hair tightening.

"Ohhh," she moaned, her head falling back into Zian's shoulder.

"A glorious sound, but not what we're looking for," he said, his touch moving to her backside to touch her in a place we hadn't explored yet. "Maybe we should just take your ass instead." Her body jolted, telling me he'd just slid at least one finger inside her. "Or better yet, maybe I'll fuck you from behind while Sorin takes your pussy. Break both virginal barriers at once and prove you can handle us. Is that what you want, sweet bird?"

She groaned, her skin pebbling with anticipation. "Yes," she whispered. "Yes."

"To which part?" he asked, his arm wrapping around her middle while his opposite hand continued to ready her in that expert way of his.

I focused on licking her to completion, her tight sheath already expanded from his previous touch. It would still hurt, her smaller frame not acquainted yet with the male form, but I'd ease her into it. Make her fall apart around my shaft. Then continue to fuck her until she begged me to stop.

It'd been too long since my last experience in a tight, wet cunt.

I intended to make this last for as long as possible.

"Raven." A lethal warning lurked in Zian's tone. "Tell us what you want and be explicit." She flinched at whatever he did behind her, likely the addition of another finger. "Because I don't think you're ready to take us at the same time. I don't think you're ready to experience the beauty of being fucked from both ends. Not yet."

She quivered, her lips parting as my tongue circled her clit once more. "I want it." She practically panted the words. "I want you both. Please."

"More," Zian encouraged. "Explicit, sweet bird. Every detail."

Her thighs began to shake, her pleasure mounting from my sweet torture below. I considered letting her shatter but instead pulled back to blow against her sensitive folds. "You heard him, baby. Tell us exactly what you want, or I'll just finish you with my tongue before Zian and I fuck around."

A soft curse fell from her sweet lips, amusing me.

She hated this game.

But it was necessary all the same.

We weren't just asking her to accept our cocks, but our bonds as well. Because we were too compatible as a trio for the mating connection not to lock into place. And once it did, there would be no going back for any of us.

Zian and I had already decided to accept it. It was too rare an occasion to turn down, and Raven needed the protection. We also couldn't deny the inexplicable need to see this through, the draw from our souls to take her into our own.

Novak would shake his head in disapproval, tell us we were binding ourselves prematurely.

Maybe we were, but it was our mistake to make.

Besides, our spirits often spoke for us in these situations. Fate's way of ensuring that angelic kind continued.

"I…" Raven paused, her tongue slipping out to dampen her lips. "I want you both inside me. I'm ready."

"Inside where?" Zian pressed.

"My soul," she whispered.

It was the right answer.

We didn't need the specifics on how or who took which part of her, just that she accepted our claim and wanted to see it fulfilled.

"Then you're going to do exactly what I say," Zian replied with a kiss against her neck. "Understood?"

She nodded. "Yes."

"Good. Then take off Sorin's—"

A blast sounded in the hallway, shaking the bed beside us and causing our door to crash open against the wall.

I spun around onto my feet, my wings flaring outward protectively.

Then my jaw hit the floor.

"Is that the outside?" I asked, seeing the massive hole in the wall.

Angels were already flying through it, escape at the forefront of everyone's mind. But I knew better than to believe it could be that easy. Nor would I ever leave without Novak at our side.

Raven darted out around me, her expression morphing into one of wonder as she watched a Noir take flight just beyond the hole.

I shared a gaze with Zian, realization striking us both at the same time.

Now was the part of our fate where we had to choose.

Except our decision was made the moment Novak went to solitary. We were brothers. "I'm not leaving him," Zian said.

"I know," I replied.

Which left Raven to make her own decision.

Either she stayed with us or she fled with the others.

CHAPTER FIFTEEN

RAVEN

ESCAPE.

The word hung in my mind like a diamond just out of reach.

I watched Noir after Noir fling themselves into the fresh hole in the wall near our open door, disappearing into the foggy sunset to freedom.

It can't be that easy, can it?

My wings flared as I burst through our open cell door. Survival came first, and it sang for me now with renewed hope, driving me forward.

Except, something was wrong.

I can't just leave.

A twist in my chest halted me in my tracks. I peeked over my shoulder, lowering a wing to find Zian and Sorin watching me. Everything in their body stances said they weren't going anywhere. Fists clenched. Jaws pulsing. Their eyes on me with a sense of resignation.

Why?

"We can't leave without Novak," Zian explained from inside our cell. He glanced at the opening, where Noir were fighting each other to squeeze through. "You're fast enough, sweet bird. You can slip through before the rest of the prison realizes there's a way out."

I swallowed the lump in my throat. Just moments ago we were all ready to bind ourselves as one for eternity, and now he wanted me to leave?

"I'm not going anywhere without you," I said, returning to them and putting my hands on theirs. I needed a physical connection to reassure myself that what we had was real and I hadn't just imagined it. "I meant it when I said I want you in my soul." My gaze flicked between his and Sorin's. "If you're staying, then I'm staying, too."

Sorin took my chin and leaned down to kiss me. "You should go, little dove." Pain flickered in his sapphire eyes, his sense of loss radiating from his expression. "You have a choice now, and I won't hold you back from making the right one."

It took me a moment to understand what he meant.

Then I followed.

He thought the right choice was to leave. *You have a choice now.* That implied I didn't have one before because we were all stuck in a cell together with our compatible hormones playing tricks on each other. So, okay, yeah, maybe that was how this had all started, but it wasn't how this was meant to end.

"No," I snapped, grabbing on to his bicep to hoist myself up to slam my lips against his. I bit down in punishment, earning a soft chuckle from my tattooed Noir. "I always had a choice." Even if the other one had been to die, it was still a choice.

"You were trapped in a cell with us," Zian softly reprimanded. "An entire prison of males wanted to tear you to pieces and devour you whole. We could have done the same, but we chose to be your protectors if you would have us. You didn't have a choice at all."

"It's called fate," I argued, wanting to slap him across

the face. I'd never believed in fate, not until I'd fallen into sin with Sorin and Zian. "I don't care if there's an airship with a big sign that says FREEDOM on it. If you're staying, then so am I, because you are my *chosen* mates."

There, I'd admitted it out loud to both of them and to myself. This wasn't just a circumstance for me.

This was real.

Relief made both of them relax, and Zian slipped an arm around my waist, bringing his lips to mine to give me an uncharacteristically sweet caress with his tongue.

When he pulled away, he raked his appreciative gaze over me, his lips curling. "While I adore you naked, maybe clothes would be a good idea until we figure out what's happening."

Right. Good plan. With a blush, I yanked on a pair of jeans and found a way to tie my top around my neck again. Just as I finished, another explosion rocked the compound, and a monstrous screech made my feathers spike.

I looked up to find the hole blown wide open, revealing that it wasn't a path to freedom at all. But one that led directly to hell.

Feathers and bones fell from a massive creature's maw—a wolf, by the looks of it. Flames and blood decorated its fur, marking it as a paranormal creature unlike anything I'd ever seen.

"A CorpseSnare," said Zian with awe in his tone. Then his wide eyes went to me, and I could see the entire scenario run through his mind.

Yeah, had I not chosen to be their mate, I would have been total dog chow.

"Raven!" Sorin shouted as he jerked me back by the arm, pulling me out of the way of a falling stone that would have crushed me into a Raven-shaped pancake. Debris rained down, making me yelp as tiny rocks pelted my shoulders and wings.

Pieces of the compound crumbled all around us as chaos erupted, the CorpseSnare chomping at nearby Noir who were dumb enough to try to get around it and pursue escape. A plethora of smaller creatures filtered into the ward, leaving death and destruction in their wake. Noir ran straight into the attack, heedless of any strategy as they mindlessly tried to fly toward false freedom.

Idiots.

"It's another culling," I hissed. "They're culling this whole damn block!"

A panicked sensation against my senses made me turn around. I found Mousey Mouse poking his nose out of our cell wall.

"What's that, Mousey Mouse?" I asked. "You found a safe place?"

Good, because we needed one. Monsters infiltrated our cell, forcing us out so we could better defend ourselves and not become cornered. Moments after battling our way outside, the entire segment collapsed, reducing our tattered mattresses to ash.

I'd almost died—*again.*

Zian cursed as he dodged a smaller creature that left a trail of inky blackness behind it. He deflected another, sending the monster smashing into an inmate. Vicious little teeth clamped down on the poor Noir's wing, making a crunching sound followed by a shriek of agony.

"We need to head toward the wolfie," I said, pointing at the massive creature gnawing on a headless body.

"Wolfie?" Zian repeated incredulously. "We encounter a deadly CorpseSnare, a creature of legends, and you nickname it *wolfie*?"

An ink creature dove for Sorin. Instead of dodging, he punched it right between the eyes, and I watched it fall to the floor in an undignified plop. Sorin sniffed at it, clearly disgusted as he lifted his lip. "Why are you asking us to run *toward* death, little dove?"

I wouldn't have noticed it even with my keen eyesight, but now that I knew what I was looking for, I spotted the tunnel that the destruction had uncovered. It would be much easier to defend than our wide-open cell room had been. I gestured at it. "There's a safe place we can hide."

More creatures continued to pour into the prison, and the wolfie thing Zian had called a CorpseSnare looked like it was almost done with his snack. Its massive jaw worked at a remaining wing, catching against thick black feathers that stuck through its teeth.

"We, uh, should try to maneuver around it while it's, um, occupied." A shiver ran up my spine. I didn't dare try to touch minds with that *thing*.

Sorin evaluated the situation, seeing the same thing we all were—chaos. Massive destruction and certain death if we didn't find someplace to hide soon.

The other cells weren't an option. The inky creatures dove into them, chomping at the trapped inmates and releasing fresh screams into the air.

I spotted the Valkyries blazing their way through the carnage. Their wild eyes said they were having the time of their lives right now. Kudos to them. Crazy bitches.

Zian grabbed me by the arm. "Lead the way."

My feathers puffed out with a slight sense of pride. It felt good to be useful, to be needed.

I spread my wings and jetted toward the tunnel's opening, dodging creatures and panicked Noir that didn't know where to go.

My nostrils flared against the burnt, mangy-dog smell as we drew close to the CorpseSnare. It was still chowing down, using its massive paw to keep part of its meal pinned as it ripped off the other wing. It must have decided it didn't like eating the feathers as it spat the wing out.

Its wild orange eyes locked on me the moment I zipped past it, and it growled.

Shit.

"Hurry!" I shouted, diving straight for the tunnel. Once inside the tight space, I found the inner corridor opened into a wide room filled with wooden boxes. Some storage unit, I supposed, but that meant there was no way out.

I turned to find Zian making his way through the tunnel, but Sorin was still trapped on the other side of the CorpseSnare. My heart jumped into my throat when the wolf decided it was tired of its meal and snarled at my tattooed angel.

"Sorin!" I shouted, and I flexed my plumes, ready to

charge back out there—not that I would be of much assistance against a supernatural wolf that boasted flames along its fur—but I couldn't leave him to fend for himself!

A brilliant blast of light caught me off guard, and I shielded my eyes just as the CorpseSnare released a shriek of pain. When I opened my eyes again and blinked away the dots scattering my vision, I found Sorin scrambling in to join us. Outside, a wall of Nora guards rained down bullets and grenade explosions against the creatures.

Why are they helping us?

"Somebody do a survival count!" came a shout, and I spotted a tall man with the burnt end of a cigarette sticking out of his mouth. He spat it out and dug in his trench coat for another. "And clean this shit up!" When no one immediately responded, he punched one of the guards in the face, sending him reeling to the ground. "Now! You useless sons of bitches!"

"Yes, sir, Warden, sir!" several voices shouted.

"I'm going to fucking kill that bitch Brina for this," the Warden muttered, shaking his head.

Sorin went still at the mention of his torturer. He still hadn't talked about it and we hadn't asked, but I'd healed his wings. I knew the extent of pain he'd been subjected to. Reaching out, I took Sorin's hand, making him flinch back to the present. "You okay?"

He gave me one of his seductive smirks, but the light still hadn't returned to his eyes. "Don't worry about me, little dove." He brought my fingers to his lips. "Looks like you saved our lives. We owe you one, and you know I don't like staying in debt long." The wink he gave me made all the heat flush to a place between my thighs.

Nora guards did a sweep with strange humming devices, taking out the creatures that had been unleashed onto the block. The three of us stayed put in the dark storage room, but we were eventually found.

"Got three here!" shouted a guard without wings as he pointed a grenade launcher at us. "Come on out or I'll just add you to the death toll."

With no other choice, we crawled out and were

immediately apprehended. My eyes went wide to find the CorpseSnare still here but being pinned down by three Nora and two non-angel guards. They were using an electrified rope as best they could, the angels flying in unison, looping and dashing to stay out of the wolf's giant, snapping mouth, while the non-angels stayed on the ground to help nail things into the concrete.

One of the wingless guards stepped too close, and all it took was one crunch to separate his head from his body.

Blood sprayed all over the Warden, who didn't even flinch. He simply lit up his cigarette and watched the remaining guards try to wrangle the beast. He would have looked calm had his cigarette not been shaking.

With the ropes pinned to the ground, the wolf whined and finally submitted, resting its bloodied snout onto a massive paw.

A heaving Nora covered in dirt and blood stalked up to the Warden, his massive wings flared out in an aggressive stance. "That thing is *your* pet! I didn't see you losing your head trying to subdue it!"

The Warden shrugged, taking a long drag from his cigarette. "Thank you for your service, Nora, and don't forget your place."

Who is this guy?

The guard seethed and stabbed a finger into the Warden's chest, making the tall man's eyes flicker with danger. "The Reformer is going to hear of this!"

That made the Warden's jaw tick. "Get the fuck out of my face."

I didn't get to hear the rest because a group of Nora redirected us toward the mass of rubble. They silently worked as they erected two poles that lit up an electric current between them. Then the Nora barked orders as they started funneling survivors through it.

"It's a portal," Sorin said, his voice low as we were shoved along.

Zian's wing brushed mine, and his body leaned into me in a protective stance. "You think they're transferring us?"

Sorin nodded.

So this massacre hadn't been intentional, not exactly.

Wherever we were going, I had a feeling that things were about to get much worse than they already were.

CHAPTER SIXTEEN

ZIAN

SHE STAYED.

Those two words rolled through my mind on repeat as we were escorted through Nightmare Penitentiary's various wards.

Per the Warden, ours was no longer habitable. He charged a handful of Nora to lead the way.

And here we were, passing through portal after portal in search of an upgraded Noir Reformatory.

Whatever the fuck that meant.

The Warden had been pissed when he found our current habitat reduced to shambles, the majority of the Noir inside dead thanks to that raging beast creature. If Mousey Mouse hadn't found us a place to hide…

I shuddered, refusing to think further about what could have happened and instead recalled the Warden's horrified expression as he brought his insane pet to heel.

And the mention of *the Reformer.*

I'd bring it up to Sorin once we were alone again.

After I kissed the hell out of him and Raven.

We'd survived.

Together.

Because she stayed. Not that she would have been able to truly escape. But she hadn't even tried, her loyalty belonging to us.

I wanted to say something. To thank her. To claim her. To shove her up against a wall and kiss her.

Yet I moved along behind her in silence, protecting her precious feathers from our ever-changing surroundings. Each ward boasted different climates and surroundings, confirming that this place was a fucking maze of nightmarish proportions.

We stepped through another portal.

Down a damp corridor lined with green moss.

Into a dungeon boasting walls of chains.

And through yet another portal that released us into a courtyard littered with charred, boulder-like rocks. A midnight sky glittered with stars overhead, providing a false sense of freedom. We all knew better than to try flying.

Beyond the yard was another corridor, this one dotted with doors.

The Valkyries led the way with a pair of Nora at the front. Two more took up the rear behind me.

A chain of about twenty Noir marched in between.

All of us silent. Exhausted. Done with these wicked games.

However, something told me the fun was just beginning, this new ward filled with puzzles and horrors just waiting for us to play.

"In you go," a Nora guard said, shoving the trio of Valkyries into a cell together. They hissed at him for daring to touch them without permission, and he grunted in reply. "Chill. If I wanted pussy, I'd take the pretty female at the back over your lot."

Raven's feathers twitched, the only sign she'd overheard.

Try it, I thought at the guard. *And you'll fucking regret it.*

Fortunately, he didn't comment further or make any move other than to usher the three of us into our new quarters.

Which contained only three walls.

The fourth was wide-open air overlooking a watery cliff. I frowned at it, certain I couldn't be seeing this right.

"Static electricity," Raven said, her enhanced eyesight allowing her to see what we couldn't. "The barriers in the frame will fry us a—"

A high-pitched shriek sounded from another cell just as our door slammed shut.

Some idiot had tried for the window.

I sighed, not even bothering to comment, and took in the mattress strewn haphazardly across the floor. A sink, a toilet, and a shower were in the corner, leaving the rest of our new home quite bare apart from a handful of sheets and pillows.

"Someone decorated in a hurry," Sorin murmured, his amusement palpable.

I glanced around at the walls and ceiling, noting the lack of surveillance. "Am I missing the obvious?" I asked, catching his gaze.

He followed my meaning, then lifted the mattress to check the ground, looked around the bathroom, and grunted. "Nothing. Guess I was right about them preparing this place fast."

"What am I not following?" Raven asked, frowning. "I mean, apart from the bland conditions."

"No cameras," I explained.

Her eyebrows lifted as she scanned the room to confirm our findings. "And a solid door with no bars."

I nodded. "No one can see us."

"Privacy," Sorin mused. "How novel. What shall we do with it?"

I knew exactly what I wanted to do with it. Raven squeaked as I threaded my fingers through her thick hair, yanked her head back, and captured her mouth in a binding kiss meant to claim completely.

She stayed.

She. Fucking. Stayed.

That decision did something to me. It unleashed a primal energy that required domination. Completion. *This.*

My sweet little bird caved on a moan, her body bowing into mine in utter submission. She knew this was it, the moment our souls joined, and I no longer needed her words to prove what she wanted because her actions already had.

Her tongue danced with mine, her nipples beading through her thin top—a top I removed with a deft flick of my fingers around her neck. She shivered, her beautiful form melting into mine as I picked up where we left off before the incident.

It didn't matter that we were exhausted.

I wanted her.

I needed to finish this.

And I could sense Sorin's desire to do the same.

Fuck time.

Fuck everything.

This was our moment, and we'd take it while we could.

He came up behind her, his hands on her waist, removing her pants as he lowered to his knees to prepare her. Her first time would hurt, but only in the best way. We'd see to her with every lick, stroke, and pet and show her what true fucking was all about.

"Unfasten my pants, sweet bird," I told her, my teeth skimming her lower lip as I drew my mouth to her ear. "Do it now."

She did, her hands shaking with anticipation as she lowered the zipper and pushed the fabric down my thighs. Her palm found my cock, giving it a stroke and making me that much harder. Then she whimpered, Sorin's tongue working magic between her thighs. I knew him well, knew he was readying her for dual penetration, his intent for me to take her ass while he fucked her tight cunt.

"You're going to be so full, baby," I whispered into her ear. "With nowhere to go, each shift of your hips only drawing us deeper inside you. Claiming you completely. Fucking you and making you truly ours."

"Yes," she hissed, her back arching to press her tits into

my bare chest.

Foreplay really wasn't needed.

All of us were primed and ready from our previous playing and the adrenaline rush brought on by our need to survive.

We *needed* this.

I kicked off my pants and took her mouth again, fucking it with the same ferocity as I intended to take her body. This wouldn't be gentle. It'd be animalistic. The way she gripped my shoulders, her nails digging into my skin, told me she could handle it. That she yearned for it as much as we did.

And then she purred, confirming every instinct inside me.

That sound was for mates.

A call to fuck her.

One I intended to answer in kind.

"She's ready," Sorin said after what felt like hours, but was probably only minutes, his lips glistening with her arousal as he stood once more behind her. He'd removed his pants, his erection bumping her hip as he moved around to her front to capture her mouth and allowed her to taste herself on his lips.

I looked on in envy, part of me dying to go to my knees for my own indulgence in that citrusy flavor that was all Raven.

But my need to be inside her won out.

"Sit on the mattress, Sorin," I demanded as I drew my hand over the head of my cock in a teasing caress. Liquid already seeped from the slit, painting my flesh in readiness. I brought it to Raven's mouth, smiling as she licked it clean with a hum of approval.

Then I grabbed her by the neck and devoured her once more, loving the way her taste mingled with Sorin's kiss and my seed. My dick pulsed, causing me to tighten my grip and kiss her even harder.

Sorin's growl made me smile, his lust so incredibly palpable when denied.

I almost made him wait a little longer, but he grabbed Raven's hand and gave her a tug. "Straddle me, little dove.

I need to be inside you."

I released her because I could and grinned as she obeyed Sorin without question, going to her knees on either side of his hips. "Fast or slow?" I wondered out loud, my question more for him than for Raven.

"Slow," he murmured. "She's very tight."

With a nod, I went to kneel behind her, my hands finding her waist to help guide her. "Reach between your thighs, sweet bird, and put Sorin's cock at your entrance." I nuzzled her neck while peering over her shoulder and down her breasts to watch her follow my command.

A tremble ran through her as his head passed over her clit, that tremble morphing into a violent quake when she introduced his head to her unused channel.

"Good girl," I praised, kissing her racing pulse. "Now you're going to slowly take him inside you. It's going to pinch a little, but I promise it won't last." My eyes met Sorin's smoldering blue gaze. "And you're not going to come until I say you can."

His cheeks reddened, the only indicator he wanted to fight my demand. Then Raven derailed any effort he could have put forth to argue by sliding down onto him the way I'd instructed.

My palms remained steady on her sides, only tightening to hold her in place when she tried to shift backward. Her whimper told me it hurt, Sorin's thick cock piercing her virginity. I cooed in her ear, reassuring her that it would feel better soon.

"You feel so good, little dove," Sorin whispered, his palm gliding up her thigh to her core. He circled her needy little clit with his thumb, drawing a sharp gasp from her as I pushed her the rest of the way down. She flinched, her body at war between desire and pain as I held her in place while she acclimated to the new position. Sweat beaded on Sorin's brow, just as it did on mine. He wanted to move and I wanted to watch him move, but she needed patience.

So I kissed her shoulder and her neck, nibbled her earlobe, and reassured her with my presence at her back. Eventually her wings relaxed, her hips doing a subtle little twist to test the pressure, and then a moan slipped from her beautiful lips.

I smiled. "There. That feels good, right?"

She nodded, her throat working as she swallowed. "Yes." She gave another shift, this one drawing a growl from Sorin as he fought to remain still beneath her.

"Fuck," he muttered, one of his hands fisting at his side while the other froze against her damp curls.

With a grin, I used my grip on her waist to lift her slightly and lower her back onto him.

"*Zian.*" Now he sounded pained.

Which only amused me.

And also made me want to join him.

"Do you think you can take me, too, sweet bird?" I asked her softly, my lips by her ear again. "It's going to make you feel even fuller and may hurt a little more at first. Especially with us both inside you."

She purred once more, the sound drawing my balls up tight as she nodded. "I want you both in me. Please, Zian."

"Now, Z," Sorin added, his voice hoarse with need. "She's so fucking tight and keeps... *fuck.*" He tossed his head back, his lips parting in a way I recognized.

"Don't you dare," I told him.

He growled a curse back at me. "Raven, if you keep clenching..." His abdominal muscles flexed, his hands reaching for her hips to hold her harshly against him. Her wings fluttered against my chest, her heart rate accelerating even more, the rhythm seductive and encouraging.

I reached between us to guide my arousal to her snug little opening at her backside, my head nudging her tender rosebud. "Fast or slow, sweet bird?" I asked her. "Fast will hurt more, but it'll be over quicker. Slow is a gradual pain. However, both will end in pleasure."

Her head fell back to my shoulder, her eyes hooded. "Fast. I can take it."

I knew she could, but I wanted her preference.

"Thank fuck," Sorin breathed.

"Just wait until I'm in there with you," I told him, readying myself to drive inside her. "You're going to feel me through that thin barrier and beg me to set the pace."

He grunted, then reached up for Raven's neck and tugged her down for a kiss. He knew this would hurt and wanted to distract her.

I didn't waste time, allowing him to provide the necessary comfort while I worked my way into her tight ass. She winced and cried out, but Sorin stole the sound with his tongue, his hand slipping between them again to thumb her bundle of nerves.

Her whimpers turned to moans, her body confused by the multitude of sensations rolling through her veins. That I could sense them told me the bond was sealing, our spirits joining together as we knew they would. Nora and Noir weren't really given a choice, aside from knowing the other was a potential mate. It served as a subtle warning that pursuing the connection would likely finalize the bonds. Our souls merely took over once we gave in to our mutual lust.

I felt Sorin, too, his acceptance warming the blossoming link.

He wanted this.

Raven wanted this.

I wanted this.

And so we were joined as one, our angelic souls marrying each other in a dance as old as time itself.

Our groans mingled as I began to move, my shaft completely sheathed inside her sweet heat, the lubrication Sorin had added enough to provide the right amount of friction and pleasure for us all.

Raven's lips left Sorin's on a scream, her over-sensitized form writhing between us as we took her in harmonious shifts of our hips. Experience radiated between Sorin and me as we thrust in time with each other, providing our sweet bird with the pleasure we promised her and more.

She panted between us.

Her tits bouncing as she lifted to press her back to my chest.

Beautiful words parted her lips, most of them praised comments underlined with our names.

Sorin pumped upward while I guided her downward, trapping her intimately as we took her to new heights, drawing an orgasm from her with a few sharp drives.

But we weren't done.

Not even close.

Just as she began to resurface, we picked up the pace, drawing tears from her eyes as she swore her body couldn't handle more.

We proved her wrong within seconds, her nipples tightening in appreciation as her orange aroma heightened around us in obvious approval. "Oh, oh, oh," she repeated, the chant causing me to smile against her neck.

"That's it," I encouraged her. "Come for us again. Squeeze Sorin's cock so good that he explodes inside that beautiful cunt."

Sorin groaned.

Raven screamed.

And the two of them came in unison, his pleasure releasing on a bellow I felt vibrate in my groin. Raven shook so violently that my hands nearly slipped, but I held on, my hips bucking into hers as I chased my own ecstasy and tumbled over the edge to join them in oblivion.

Our scents mingled, a citrusy caramel cologne stealing over us, finalizing our mating in a cloud of rightness.

Mine, I thought, biting her shoulder hard enough to leave a mark. *You're mine.*

Sorin lifted to do the same to her breast, his eyes meeting mine as his teeth sank down hard enough to wound, which led to Raven falling apart a third time between us, her purr radiating loudly in stark acceptance.

We collapsed as one, my cock still throbbing inside her.

I didn't bother to pull out.

We'd be doing this again in a few minutes.

Just as soon as I caught my breath.

CHAPTER SEVENTEEN

SORIN

RAVEN LICKED THE TIP OF MY COCK, her greedy little mouth seeking every last drop of my cum after expertly sucking me off. I shuddered, my fingers tightening in her hair as I guided her down for one last thorough suck. She moaned, her own pleasure cresting as Zian pumped into her sweet pussy, spilling his seed deep inside her.

Fuck, she was perfect.

So damn beautiful, her lips releasing me with a pop as Zian wrapped his hand around her throat to guide her backward into his chest. He tilted her head to receive his kiss while I drew my lips down her neck and her pert tits to the space between her thighs where his cock still pulsed with his release.

Her little nub throbbed beneath my tongue while I forced another orgasm from her. She screamed, causing Zian to smile and nibble her lower lip. "Are you going to clean off my cock with that sexy mouth of yours?" he asked her after she came down from her high. "Or should Sorin do it?"

I grunted because I intended to lick her, not him.

"Me." She shifted, causing him to slip from inside her.

"Straddle my face, little dove," I told her, rolling to my back. "I'm not done tasting you."

She obliged me, her thighs shaking as she placed her slick folds just above my mouth. My tongue swept over her, reveling in the flavor of her pleasure mingling with Zian's cum.

"Divine," I murmured, then devoured her to completion.

She was still working on Zian when I felt her body begin to vibrate once more, her back bowing as she tried to pull her lips away from his dick—likely to tell me to stop.

He grabbed her and I latched onto her hips, driving her forward with my teeth gently nibbling her swollen flesh.

Her garbled complaint made me grin.

Then she exploded in yet another wave of ecstasy.

"Oh, sweet bird. I love how easily you come," Zian said, his shaft deep in her throat and absorbing her moans. I knew from moments ago how good those vibrations felt, as he'd brought her to climax twice while I fucked her mouth. His groan of pleasure rivaled mine, her throat working as she swallowed every drop.

He finally released her, but not before she gave him a little kiss on the head of his cock as if saying a sweet goodbye. His lips twitched at the gesture, as did mine when she collapsed beside me in a heap of feathers.

Only, a chittering sound had her bouncing right back up. Her little mouse pet appeared at the foot of the mattress. She turned to face him on her belly, resting her chin on her forearms. Sorin and I shared an amused look before mimicking her pose on either side of her, our wings fanning hers in a layer of feathery protection.

"What's he saying?" I asked, her expression intent as she listened.

"He's complaining that we mate too much," she said with a shy smile, then her expression turned serious. "He came to tell us that the demons in solitary broke out." Her eyes narrowed. "They asked Novak to go with them."

"He didn't." Zian sounded sure of it, probably because he could feel his cousin through their familial link. "He's still here."

"Yeah, Mousey Mouse says he refused." She went quiet as the mouse continued to squeak. "He thinks Novak might come back soon because the Warden is in trouble with someone higher up." She frowned. "Are you talking about *the Reformer?*"

Zian met my gaze, this time his expression holding a tense line that I understood all too well. I'd overheard the guard's comment the other day about reporting back to the notorious Nora charged with rehabilitating Noir kind. Most referring to him reverently as *the Reformer.*

I preferred calling him an almighty jackass.

But his real name was Sayir. His brother, Sefid, used to be my commander as the Royal King of the Nora. So we'd met a few times.

"Mousey Mouse doesn't know," Raven murmured. "He just says the Warden has been busy trying to make things right after what happened with the CorpseSnare, which is why we've been in our cell all week. They're creating a new Noir Reformatory around us."

"How did the demons escape?" Zian cut in.

Raven repeated the question, her brow furrowing as the mouse replied. "He isn't sure. Something about the demons finding their puzzle piece. I have no idea what he's talking about. He just keeps saying something about how they finally fit themselves back together." She shrugged. "We'll have to ask Novak what that means."

Zian snorted. "Unless it's relevant, he won't tell us."

"Yeah, he doesn't talk much." Especially not to strangers, meaning he'd be very quiet around Raven until he decided to trust her. Which could take a few decades, knowing Novak.

"What's the deal with the three of you?" she asked as the mouse disappeared, apparently out of information to share.

"Deal?" Zian repeated, resting his cheek on his forearms to better observe Raven. I did the same, mimicking his pose while she remained sandwiched between us with her chin on her folded arms.

"Yeah, like, who is he to you? Another warrior? A lover? A really good friend?"

Ah, I understood what she meant. "You're asking if he'll join our mating."

"No." Zian's tone brooked no argument, not that he'd get one from me.

Because, yeah, there was absolutely no way Novak was joining this arrangement.

Not that he would anyway.

No, something told me it'd take a very unique circumstance for Novak to ever willingly share a lover. If he had any interest in taking one at all. He rarely fucked around as a Nora, and as far as I knew, he hadn't been with anyone since becoming a Noir.

"So he's not...?" Raven trailed off, her eyebrows drawing down.

"He's like a brother to us," I explained. "He's Zian's cousin."

"And we will not be sharing you with him," Zian added in case that wasn't clear. "You're ours and ours alone."

I nodded, agreeing. "The three of us have been together for about a hundred and fifty years, give or take a few. We were Nora warriors before our Fall, which formed a sort of impenetrable bond. Then Zian and I improved upon that bond over the years."

"He means we started sharing women and fucking each other." Zian, always the blunt bastard, just had to go make Raven blush.

Which she did. "So I'm not the first you've shared."

I arched a brow at him, encouraging him to continue down that road since he turned the conversation to that path.

"There have been a few," he answered vaguely. "But you're the only one we've ever claimed."

Smooth, I thought, nearly rolling my eyes. I really hoped

she didn't ask him to define *a few*. Something told me her definition would vary significantly from his.

He leaned in to kiss his mark against her neck before she could reply, and a zing of electricity swept over the three of us. His mouth had left a navy blue pattern against her skin, appropriate since that was his color of choice when applying ink to my skin. My bite, however, had embedded a circle of gold ink in her breast.

A heart of gold was our ongoing joke because of my knack for influencing trust in others. Really, I was just hyperaware of everyone's motives. That was how I'd felt Raven's intentions the day we first met when she threw that blade at me. I'd anticipated the shift in the air, my instincts causing me to turn, and *wham*!

The thought would have made me growl a few weeks ago.

Today, I merely smiled.

Raven was a survivor. I could respect that, even if her survival tactic nearly led to my demise.

Zian pulled her beneath him in a clever shift of their bodies, whirling her around to her back and forcing her legs to part for his hips as he settled himself against her. "Mine," he said possessively.

"Ours," I corrected, going up onto my elbow to watch as he lazily kissed her.

We'd spent the last however many days doing this, playing and reveling in our new bond. Occasionally food appeared. We ate it and then went back to our fucking. It was a pretty common reaction to a new coupling, our desire for sex skyrocketing beyond anything I'd ever experienced in my many years of existence.

Zian slid inside her, taking her at a leisurely pace while I stroked my shaft in anticipation.

And when he finished, I took her, my mouth and thrusts a little more demanding against hers after the buildup of watching them play. She accepted everything I had to give and more, her eager walls clenching around me as I came deep inside her thoroughly fucked pussy.

She sighed, content, while Zian licked her clean this time

and I fed my cock between her lips.

Sometime later, as the sun began to set, she asked, "So is the Reformer real?"

I blinked up at the ceiling, then canted my head toward her, startled by the query. "What do you mean? Of course he's real."

Her lips curled down. "So he's not just a myth?"

Zian went to his elbow to look over her at me, his eyes conveying the same confusion I felt inside. "He's King Sefid's brother," I said slowly.

"Who's King Sefid?"

This time I sat up to study her prone form, trying to determine if she was serious or fucking with me. "King Sefid is the King of the Nora."

"There's a King of the Nora?" She seemed to consider that. "Huh. I guess that makes sense. But I just thought they were guards mostly for the prison. I never really thought much more about them or what they do."

"I'm really starting to believe your story about your wings." Zian's tone held a hint of wonder as he stroked her feathers. "The Nora are not just guards but also an entire race. They have a whole social structure, with King Sefid at the top and his warriors just below him."

"Sayir earned his nickname as *the Reformer* because he was put in charge of rehabilitating the Noir," I added. "That was a few hundred years before my time, and I used to think he was doing a good job until we ended up in the system."

Zian's expression darkened. "Now we know there is no such thing as reform. We've been left here to rot, whether we deserve it or not."

"Yeah, that's why we took over our last prison." We could have escaped, but we'd just end up back in the system. So better to own it than to flee from it. Except... "Then they sent us here." And I wasn't sure I wanted to remain in this place.

Silence fell between us, the three of us thoughtful.

"So you've never heard of King Sefid or his brother, Sayir?" Zian asked quietly after several minutes. "That's the kind of thing parents teach their Nora children about early in the youngling years."

"I didn't have parents," she replied, her voice just as soft. "I was raised in an all-female penitentiary meant for youths."

My lips parted as I again looked at Zian. "Youth prisons? For female Noir?" I'd never heard of such a place. They certainly didn't exist when I was a warrior. "I'm surprised King Sefid allowed that." Not that I really knew him anymore. I was pretty sure I never did, considering he just abandoned the three of us in the system to die for a minor infraction.

"I think it's safe to say we didn't know him at all," Zian said as if reading my mind. And maybe he had to an extent, as we could sense each other's moods through the bond.

"How did you two Fall?" Raven asked. "I mean, clearly you weren't born this way like me. You earned your black wings by doing something else. What was it?"

Earned was an interesting choice of words, but I didn't comment on it. Instead, I let Zian take the lead on replying. He told the story better, meaning he was faster and more efficient.

"Novak has an affinity for strategy, similar to my repentance magic, only more mental than physical. Anyway, we were sent after a Noir, told to take him in dead or alive, and we had the guy in our sights. Then Novak insisted on letting him go, said something wasn't right about the situation, and we chose to believe him."

"Loyalty to each other over our warriorship," I added, my voice nearing a growl. "That's what they called it when our wings turned black."

"When you take the warrior oath, you vow to protect the Nora above all else. Which includes listening to our instincts, apparently, because we were punished for not following orders."

"By all accounts, our wings should have turned back, but they never did. So we gave up trying." Perhaps that was the wrong thing to do, but we wouldn't have survived the system had we continued to play by Nora rules. Noir were a different breed. The prison also didn't make assignments based on crime level, putting everyone with black wings together and forcing them to do whatever was necessary to survive.

So we survived.

"We no longer believe in reformation." Zian shrugged. "And by proxy, we no longer believe the Reformer is doing what he set out to do." He looked down at Raven, his dark eyes smoldering. "Which is why I believe you, Raven. That you never experienced the Fall, but were born with black wings. It makes too much sense with your innocence and upbringing."

Not to mention the lack of a lie sensed through the bond, I thought but didn't add that out loud. "I wonder if Noir mates produce Noir babies," I said. The whole "sins of the parents" myth applying to children seemed almost too accurate in this situation.

"It's entirely possible," Zian agreed, his fingers strumming across her feathers again. "You were never told anything about your parents?"

She shook her head. "I only know that I grew up in the system with my black wings, and many have said I'll never escape it."

I nodded. "Well, that's probably true. Which is why we need to take over this place like we did our last prison."

"It'll be a challenge with everything shifting and moving every damn day," Zian muttered. "Not to mention the constant change in the Noir population here."

"Truth." But given what I'd seen on our transfer here, fleeing wasn't really an option. We also couldn't leave Novak behind. "It's a good thing I enjoy challenges."

Zian smirked. "Truth," he said, purposely repeating my comment. "Step one, dominate the prison. Step two, get Novak back. Step three, escape. A walk in the park."

"Except this place is a fucking maze."

"No, it's Nightmare Penitentiary," he corrected, his lips curling. "So I guess we just have to hope our dreams come true, yeah?"

"Well, one has already," I said, looking down at the beauty between us. "Several times."

Her cheeks flushed prettily, her lips parting as she knew what we intended to do next.

The same thing we'd done for days on end.

Fuck her.

Only, a sound from the door had us pausing that thought, our attention moving to the paper sliding beneath the crack from the hallway and across the floor. Zian reached for the note, unfolding it for us all to read.

And my heart sank to my stomach.

Tag, you're it, Breeder Bitch. Prepare for the next culling. I'm challenging you. —V

Either a Nora guard was fucking with us or a Valkyrie had convinced him to slip the note under our door. My gut said it was the latter.

Which meant our Raven needed to be prepared.

"Guess we should fix up a sparring area," Zian said, crumpling the note into his palm and throwing it at the electric field lighting up our back wall. The paper went up in flames before dissolving into ash.

I kissed Raven with everything I owned before saying, "Stand up, little dove. We're going to teach you how to take a few hits and then how to fight from the ground." Because I knew how this Valkyrie fought. Raven would need to know how to leverage her wings while on her back and also how to block a punch.

"I'm sorry, baby, but this is going to hurt," Zian added.

And the real training began.

CHAPTER EIGHTEEN

RAVEN

MY MATES WERE INSATIABLE IN BED.

And assholes out of it.

Okay, not really. I just didn't like them all that much at the moment. Two weeks of endless training sucked. I'd worked with Zian before, and he hadn't gone easy on me, but it had never been anything like this.

At least the aftercare was enjoyable.

My breath left me in a rush as I took Sorin's punch. He certainly didn't hold back.

I didn't want him to.

"Again," Zian demanded, his words as cold as ice, but I saw a spark in his eyes that said this hurt him more than it hurt me.

Maybe.

Sorin tossed his fist again, but things had progressed enough that this wasn't necessary anymore. I angled so that his fist hit my forearm instead of my ribs. The impact still hurt, but at least I didn't have the wind knocked out of me again.

My healing magic, now accelerated, swept over my arm with a tingling warmth that instantly worked on soothing the pain.

He smirked. "Nice deflection, but that wasn't today's exercise."

Rubbing my arm, I stuck my tongue out at him.

"Mature, Rave," Zian chided, but this time a smile lit his eyes.

"You can stop conditioning me. I can take a punch already." This kind of training could only be described as brutal and blunt, not to mention mentally hard for me to handle, but it had taught me how to use my inherent gifts efficiently and effectively.

My forearm finished mending as I retreated from our makeshift arena at the edge of the cliff. I stepped over the burn marks sweeping across the ground. They sectioned off our workout zone, which was far enough from the cliff to avoid hitting the invisible field and large enough for sparring.

In spite of my healing magic being the strongest it had ever been, my entire body ached and all I wanted to do was curl up into a ball and sleep for a year. At first, the thought of either Zian or Sorin raising a hand against me made me want to rip both their balls off, but then I realized that they saw me as an equal, as one of their clan, and wanted me to train the same way they trained each other.

Harshly.

Without mercy.

It worked. Sparring for hours on end and getting hit in places that brought tears to my eyes had triggered my healing magic to go into overdrive. I didn't have to stop and concentrate to initiate a healing. Now it came naturally.

Having my magic constantly hum over my skin wore me out, and I marched over to our mattress and collapsed onto it. I chomped down the last of yesterday's hard bread. It was technically Zian's portion, but food was the best way to maintain my energy, so he gave it all to me.

As for water, we needed more than the measly bottles tossed in by the guards every now and then. And the sink water tasted horrible. With all the sweating from fighting and sex, hydration was a must. So we gathered extra reserves in a carved-out basin Zian had made with a few loose rocks, his magic providing a unique glue of singed material. Dew and raindrops made their way into our reservoir, and I dipped my small hands into it, cupping the deliciously cool liquid and bringing it to my lips.

I peeked up to find both Sorin and Zian watching me with a sense of appreciation. They thought everything I did was fascinating.

With the sun still rising, we were nowhere near the end of our all-day training session. I knew that by nightfall, my entire body would be sore and my mood soured. Zian and Sorin always made up for it, soothing all my hurts with their kisses and caresses and massaging me in all the right places—inside and out.

Maybe I could entice them into an earlier—

A loud bang shattered my focus, followed by the dead bolt unlatching. The door swung open to reveal three guards holding chains.

One for each of us.

We complied without a word, allowing the guards to shackle our legs and put weights on our wings. The latter interested me because it meant we were going to a place in the compound that was not yet flight-proof. I raised an eyebrow at Zian, who nodded his unspoken agreement.

It might not be a chance to escape, not yet, but it meant our new ward wasn't ready. We'd find an opportunity to catch our captors when they let their guard down.

Until then, we had to focus on step one of Sorin's plan.

Dominate the prison.

I knew where we were going without being told as we fell into a single-file line, one guard at our front, one walking alongside us, and one at our back. This had to be the challenge mentioned in Vivian's letter. I'd overheard the guards talking about her and gathered that *V* was short for Vivian, not Valkyrie. Bryn and Freya were the names of the other two.

I'd have to guess which name belonged to which bitch.

Of course, *V* for Vivian would probably be the easiest bet, as she seemed to have it out for me, per her note.

Interesting that her challenge arrived two weeks later— a timeline I only knew because of Sorin's penchant for marking the wall every sunrise.

I'd begun to think Vivian's taunt was all talk, a way to toy with me beforehand. But my chains suggested it was something else entirely—the arena hadn't been ready yet.

So how did she know a challenge was coming? Did someone tell her? Or was it a guess?

I supposed it was an educated guess based on previous rituals.

"It feels strange to leave our nest," I admitted softly.

"Our cell," Zian corrected me.

Sorin smirked. "Let her call it our nest. I think it's endearing." He flashed a smile over one wing as he lowered his voice. "When we're out of here, little dove, we'll make a real nest."

A passing guard slapped him on the back of his head. "No talking," he chided, but his grin said he'd heard and was going to delight in proving Sorin wrong.

It had never occurred to me to imagine what life would be like outside of the prison environment. Sure, I thought about escape daily, but my imagination never went any further than picturing myself soaring above the clouds, free and flying without worrying about anything. I wanted to be so far away from Nora guards and untrustworthy inmates that I no longer listed *survival* as my top priority.

I dreamt of a place where I could actually *live*.

But what did that mean, exactly? Before, it had meant the simplicity of freedom. Now? Now, it meant a life with Sorin and Zian.

A real life.

It wasn't something I could picture in my head, but neither were most of the pleasurable acts my mates had taught me. They could show me what life was supposed to be like, and that realization made my heart flutter with excitement.

My elation died as quickly as it had materialized when we stepped out into a courtyard filled with sharp black rocks that lacerated my bare feet. My healing magic activated, working to close the wounds as soon as I lifted off of each step, but the rush of pain made me dizzy.

Delving into that warm place in my chest where I retreated to during the endless training sessions with Sorin and Zian, I found a way to escape the pain. We hadn't even started today's culling challenge, and I was already having to make use of what I'd learned.

Much of the courtyard was a wide-open expanse that overlooked the sea, telling me that we had relocated to another side of the massive island. Waves crashed against black cliffs, offering a symphony of nature's violence to the ambience.

A few minutes' trek brought us to a netted area that was clearly a temporary housing unit for today's challenge. Inmates crammed in against one another while leaving the far end open. I saw why when the guards shoved us in and closed off the gate behind us, flipping a switch that electrified the netting.

Dueling rings waited for us, and guards funneled inmates in one by one. I couldn't spot the electrified wiring that should have sectioned them off, but the inmates weren't taking chances and stayed well within the boundaries.

I spotted the Valkyries waltzing among the inmates like they owned all of them. The males were as dumb as ever, fawning all over the female warriors, hoping to get a taste of their sensual violence. Maybe they didn't care if the Valkyries would kill them—at least they'd have sex first.

"Pathetic," I whispered harshly under my breath, earning a chuckle from Sorin. He shrugged off the chains on his wings after the guard undid them. Then he flexed his magnificent plumes, expertly scanning the crowded courtyard before locking gazes with the tallest of the Valkyries. She grinned at him, running her tongue suggestively over her lips.

"You're not going anywhere near her," I said, my words a threat.

As if in response to my demand, the Valkyrie said something to one of the guards, and he grinned before going straight for Sorin.

Against my better judgment, I put myself between Sorin and the Nora as I flared my smaller, more delicate wings—now also free of their chains—in an attempt to look threatening.

The approaching guard raked his gaze over me. My once thin clothes were already hopelessly tattered, leaving little to the imagination. The fact that the guards hadn't given me new clothes suggested they enjoyed the view a bit too much. "Move. The male has been challenged." He jerked his thumb to indicate the dueling rings. "Unless you want to take Freya's place?"

Ah, so you're Freya. Good to know, Tall Bitch.

It annoyed me that the guards had learned the Valkyries' names but called the rest of us "inmate" or worse. It indicated that the warrior females were already well on their way to dominating a prison that should be ours.

The guard grinned, looking between me and Sorin. "It would be entertaining to see if he would risk Brina's blade by letting you live again, now that he knows what he's in for." He shrugged. "But I did promise him to Freya, so maybe we can save that for next time if you both survive."

Sorin put a warm hand on my hip, making my wings shrink as he leaned in to whisper in my ear. "I can take care of myself, little dove. You just remember everything we taught you."

It took all of my willpower to step out of the way as the guard toted him off to a smug-looking Freya, who grinned at me with her hands propped on her hips.

Bitch.

I didn't get to see who Zian would have to face because a different guard grabbed me roughly by the arm and dragged me toward another one of the rings with a Valkyrie waiting inside.

So this must be Vivian, I thought. *Awesome.*

She ran her delicate fingers over a blade as she paced her end of the ring. Her pointed teeth made her look a bit wild, as did the crazed gleam in her eyes. The guard released me and stepped out of the boundary lines.

"Where's my weapon?" I snapped, which earned a shrug from the guard.

"What's the matter?" Vivian asked, delight caressing every word that slithered from her mouth. "Scared?"

"I thought you wanted a real challenge." I narrowed my eyes. It didn't matter how much training I'd been through with Zian and Sorin; if the fight was already rigged, then I was doomed.

"That's why I gave you a warning," she countered, blinking her big eyes at me innocently as she paced. "You're mentored by two of the finest warriors here, are you not? Surely they taught you how to disarm an opponent." She licked the edge of her blade, leaving a trail of blood and making me grimace. Her gaze went to Sorin, who curled his fingers into fists and faced Freya. "We're going to have so much fun with them once you're gone."

That made me see red.

Or at least, I thought it had until I felt heat explode in the air around us. Literal flames shot up from the boundary of our fighting ring, blocking out my view of anyone or anything outside.

Vivian's eyes flared with excitement as she dipped the sword into the inferno. It must have been coated with something because it came back billowing with flames along its edge. "Looks like it's time to play."

She flared her wings, bursting toward me with a rush of speed I was unaccustomed to when sparring with my lovers. I reacted out of instinct and dodged enough to miss a fatal blow, but her weapon still grazed me. Pain seared across my rib cage where the flames licked across my skin, catching my top on fire.

Screeching as blisters ran up my neck, I ripped off my clothes before she could use the fabric to burn me alive. My vision went hazy as pain engulfed me, the slice of steel paired with liquid heat making my body want to shut down.

There wasn't time to rest. The inferno walls of our ring closed in on us, making panic surge in my chest.

"Looks like the guards want me to kill you off quickly," she said with a sneer. "A pity. You're such a pretty little breeder, and I wanted to take my time marking up your face." Her blade lunged at me again, this time going for my wings.

I launched out of the way as a flash of heat ran up my softer plumes. My healing magic worked in the background, dissipating the blisters and keeping my feathers from catching fire.

She clicked her tongue. "Impressive. The bitch has a few tricks." She stabbed her blade into the ground as the wall of flames stopped advancing on us, the ring already too small for a proper fight. She grinned, facing me with just her fists. "I wonder how your mates take you. Is it like this?"

There wasn't time to dodge, not with her movements lightning fast as she rammed me and pinned me to the ground, my head inches away from the wall of flames that encompassed our small arena. Her hands went to my throat, and I clawed at her wrists as her sharp nails dug into my skin. I took in a gasp of air before she cut off my airway.

She ground her hips into mine, lewdly mimicking thrusts. "Do they like to mount you like this? It's far too easy. You're just a breeder in heat. Such fine warriors need a real challenge." She grinned, flashing those awful teeth again. "I bet Freya is fucking your tattooed one right now. He's got to be tired of you." She thrust her hips again, chafing hard leather against my raw skin. "Maybe he'll get off on it if he hears you scream before you die."

She made the mistake of loosening her grip as she rolled her hips against me. I sensed Zian in my mind a moment before a flash of silver cut through the inferno—his magic burned the edges. I caught the item in midair. I couldn't see him, but maybe he could somehow see me and he'd just tossed me a weapon.

I hoped that meant his opponent was dead, but there wasn't time to fret over my mates. Instead, I twisted and wasted no time sinking the blade into the side of the Valkyrie's neck.

Her eyes went wide on a gasp as she clawed at the hilt, and soon her head lolled back as a horrid gurgle sounded from her throat.

I heaved in gulps of hot air as I rubbed the bruises blossoming across my throat. My healing magic worked on it instantly, soothing the ache of a nearly crushed windpipe.

My heart thundered in my chest as water doused the flames and revealed the rest of the survivors.

Zian was nowhere to be found, but I spotted a Noir with his heart missing from his chest in one of the nearby rings.

Sorin watched me as his chest heaved, shimmering against the sunlight from the sweat and blood coating him. The color matched his rage that filtered through our mate-bond.

One more set of eyes was on me, and I glanced up to find the last surviving Valkyrie seething, every muscle in her body locked tight as she likely plotted all the ways she could dismember me while my mates watched.

Good. We'd pissed off the youngest of the Valkyrie circle. Something told me she was the most violent of them all, her expression void of any emotion except vengeance.

Two down, one to go.

Hello, Bryn.

You're next.

CHAPTER NINETEEN

SORIN

"I REALLY NEED PEOPLE to stop fucking with my wings," I muttered as I returned to the cell with Raven right in front of me.

"But you like when I play with your feathers." Zian was sprawled out on the bed, his hair mussed but otherwise resembling his usual warrior perfection.

His sensual comment made my lips curl. Because, yeah, I did enjoy it when he stroked my wings.

"Did you at least wash your hands after that display?" I asked, heading over to the shower to clean Freya's death off my skin. Raven joined me without a word, her palms stroking my burnt plumes and igniting a warming energy between us that seemed to go straight to my dick.

I pressed a fist to the wall, groaning in both pleasure and agony as the feathers mended themselves.

"That sounds like an invitation," Zian mused, moving gracefully to his feet and shucking off his jeans. Mine were destroyed in the fire. Same with Raven's clothes. The prison would provide us with a new wardrobe at some point.

"And yes, I already washed off," Zian added, stepping up to stroke a finger down Raven's spine. "I wouldn't want to spill any blood on our sweet little bird."

She snorted, glancing over her shoulder. "Why not? I'm already covered in Valkyrie bitch."

Oh, someone was riled up. I hadn't seen much of her match, too busy fighting off the female who seemed hell-bent on fucking me, burning me, and killing me, all at once.

Taking down a woman felt wrong when I knew how few existed.

But that Valkyrie cunt had earned her death and then some.

As soon as the fiery walls of the ring went up into the sky, she'd shoved me. Hence my wounded wings. Then she'd attempted to mount me, and I saw red.

Only two angels in my life were allowed that privilege, and they were both sharing the shower with me right now.

I turned to place my hands on the wall, giving Raven my back so she could better access my wings. She immediately homed in on the other areas that required mending, her touch sizzling my nerves in the best way.

"You fought well," Zian murmured, his words for Raven. He'd gone through the first round of the challenges, decimating his opponent in less than a minute and ripping the poor bastard's heart out before smashing it between his teeth like some sort of monstrous animal.

I hated it when he did that, but the tactic worked. Everyone gave him a wide berth, even the newbies.

"You could see me?" Raven asked, her fingers combing through my feathers, searching for any other blemishes to heal. "I couldn't see anything beyond the flames."

I frowned at her statement. *What?* I'd been able to see through the inferno from both sides.

"Yeah, they were translucent," Zian said slowly. "Weren't you able to see me and Sorin in our rings?"

She shook her head. "No, just fire."

"Interesting." Zian's inflection didn't match the word.

155

"Must be something with the infrared?"

That question was for me. I could tell by the lethal edge lurking in his tone. He wanted my opinion and hoped I'd give him a favorable one.

Unfortunately, my mind went elsewhere.

"Or they've found a way to disable her visual advantage," I replied, not pleased by that notion at all. "We'll need to find a way to test that."

"Yeah." His tone rivaled my opinions on it.

Raven needed every edge she could find to stay ahead and couldn't afford to become more vulnerable than she already was in a prison full of hungry males. They wouldn't care at all that we'd mated her. If anything, it'd only inspire them to try harder because she now resembled a weakness in our armor. Hurting her would hurt us.

"I'm fine, guys," she mumbled, her palms caressing my fully healed plumes. "But I'll keep my eyes open and see if I notice any other differences."

"In the interim, have you noticed our cell enhancements?" Zian asked, his chin gradually shifting to the left, toward a corner near our open wall of electricity.

I turned around to face Raven, then dipped my head back into the spray of the shower to dampen my hair. As I used the soap to create suds against the strands, I surveyed the "enhancements" Zian mentioned.

A new camera.

Awesome.

After rinsing the makeshift shampoo from my long hair, I took another lazy perusal of the room and noted the lack of listening devices. Apparently, they were still only interested in watching. "I wonder if all the cells are under surveillance or if the Nora guards chose ours because they like looking at our pretty little Raven?"

"I'm going to assume that's your way of telling me there's no one listening to us."

I smirked. "You'd assume right, Z."

He nodded. "That was my assessment."

"Why are they only watching us?" Raven asked. "I mean, I get their interest in our, uh, mating. But I feel like there's more to it. Like why are they letting us just fuck around? I thought they'd use this against us somehow."

"They will," I said, turning off the water after giving Raven a thorough rinse. "But not for a bit."

"Not until you go into heat," Zian added, following my train of thought like he always seemed to do. "They'll separate us then, and it'll suck. Majorly."

I nodded. "Especially if they try to let someone else satisfy your urges. A lot of Noir are going to die when that happens."

"Hopefully, we have a few years or decades. Nora go into heat, what, once every six or seven years? No idea on Noir, and as you seem to have been born this way…" He trailed off, leaving the rest unsaid. Because we didn't know what would happen.

"Vivian accused me of already being in heat," Raven said as we pulled her down to the mattress with us. "Said I was fucking the two of you like a breeder begging for, uh, well, you know."

Yeah, I did. I'd overheard that taunt before the other Valkyrie tried to burn me alive. "You're not in heat."

"How can you be so sure? We've been all over each other."

Zian chuckled. "That's called mating lust, sweet bird."

"If you were in heat, we'd be in pain every moment we weren't fucking you," I explained. "It's like an animalistic requirement to impregnate a mate in heat. We'll be incapable of doing anything other than taking turns coming all over you."

"And inside you," Zian murmured.

"Yeah, definitely inside you," I agreed.

"Are you sure that's not what we've been doing?" she asked, her tone genuine. "I mean, you two have taken me repeatedly for weeks."

"To stake our claim." Zian tucked her hair behind her ear and balanced himself on an elbow beside her. I copied his position on her opposite side, both of us staring down at her on her back.

"You're ours, little dove." I leaned in to nuzzle her neck

and give her pulse a sweet nip. "We want the entire prison to know it."

"So I'm not going to get pregnant."

"Not today or anytime soon," I confirmed, drawing my nose along her jaw to her lips. "Trust me, you'll know. You'll cramp with a need so intense you'll hardly be able to walk, if at all."

"And you'll demand us to take you in every manner possible." Zian murmured the words directly against her ear, drawing goose bumps along her neck and arms. "It'll be glorious, sweet dove. Just thinking about it makes me so fucking hard for you."

I chuckled against her throat, drawing my teeth downward to her collarbone to skip across it and onward to her breast. She bowed off the mattress as I taunted her stiff peak with my tongue, Zian's hand cupping her between her thighs.

"Are you in the mood for a demonstration, sweet bird?" he asked. "Do you want to feel how efficiently and thoroughly we'll take you?"

"Mmm, after winning that challenge, I'd say she more than deserves a little attention." I sucked her nipple deep, then smiled as her citrusy arousal sharpened around us. "I think that's a yes, Z."

"It's absolutely a yes," he agreed, joining me to torment her other taut bud.

Then together we went down, taking turns with our mouths against her intimate flesh until she swore she couldn't take any more.

Only then did we take her, me at the back and Zian at the front, our cocks moving in unison and drawing yet another orgasm from her.

"Your snug little cunt is killing me," Zian groaned, his pace quickening as he found his release inside her.

I joined him after a few harsh thrusts of my own, her tight backside squeezing every last drop from my shaft until I collapsed against her shoulder, my breaths coming in pants against her dewy skin.

"I'm…" She paused, inhaling sharply. "Totally in heat,"

she finished.

I grinned. "No, little dove. Because if you were, you would have never begged us to stop licking you."

"He's right," Zian murmured, tangling his fingers in her hair to angle her face upward to receive his kiss. "You would have told us to never stop," he added after a long moment of thoroughly taking her mouth.

He released her, allowing me to do the same, tugging her backward to meet my waiting lips.

She smiled when I finished, her cheeks flushed, her body pulsating beautifully between us. "Will it always be like this?"

"No, sweet bird," Zian said, nuzzling her neck. "It only gets better."

"And better," I added, giving her hips a tentative thrust.

When she moaned in response, I knew she could take more.

So we coaxed her slowly into another round, her supple form taking everything we had to give, until the three of us were beyond satisfied and collapsed in a pile of sweaty limbs on the mattress.

She snuggled into me, her head on my shoulder, while Zian cocooned her from behind.

And we fell into a blissful sleep.

Until a scratching noise woke us up, the mouse appearing with a warning, something about the prison being rebuilt to suit the Noir's needs. Whatever the fuck that meant. The little mouse disappeared to check on Novak, per Zian's request, leaving the three of us to ponder over the future.

"We need to get out of here," Zian said, doing that thing where he read my mind despite it being an impossible skill. "But not without Novak."

I scratched my jaw, considering our surroundings and what I knew about the penitentiary. "Yeah, this place is a fucking maze." Pretty sure I'd said that already. The opinion hadn't changed one bit.

"Then we should start trying to map it out." Zian sat up, his wings pulled tight into his back. "We need to be prepared when Novak returns. His knack for strategy will come in handy, and he may have learned something from the demons who managed to escape solitary. Since the rat says they haven't been recaptured, it's safe to assume their tactic worked."

"Mouse," Raven corrected. "And just because he hasn't seen them again doesn't mean they weren't killed or put somewhere else."

"True," I agreed. "But your pet hasn't seen them anywhere, and it seems like he knows his way around the prison."

Zian's eyes widened. "We need to use him—the *mouse*. He can help us map out the wards."

"Only if you promise not to eat him," Raven replied, arching a dark brow.

Zian smirked. "If he continues being useful, then sure."

My lips twitched. That little rodent was probably the safest pet in this prison because Zian would die before he touched something Raven deemed precious. He might tease, but I knew him well. He would protect that rodent almost as fiercely as he did her, if only to ensure her happiness.

"If they give us flight time tomorrow, I want to survey the water and the cliffs, get a good handle on what's happening in the ocean around us," Zian added, ever the planner. I swore it ran in his blood as a result of his familial ties to Novak. The two of them were similar in so many ways, yet not in several others.

Raven nodded. "I'll help."

"No, you'll be training with Sorin tomorrow." He leaned down, cupping her cheek when she began to sputter an argument. "I saw the way Bryn looked at you during that fight, sweet bird. You took on one of her sisters, and Sorin killed the other. She might be the youngest of the trio, but she seems to be the most dangerous of them all. And now she wants revenge."

He was right. I'd caught her angry expression, and it had been directed at Raven, not at me.

Zian finished his lecture with a kiss, one that encouraged

her compliance, which she eagerly gave. She wasn't one of those females who argued for the sake of arguing. If she understood the purpose, she usually accepted it. And if she disagreed, she voiced her reason.

I loved that about her.

Loved that she allowed us to protect her while equally protecting herself.

It created the perfect dynamic between us, one that would hopefully keep us all alive long enough to find a way out of this nightmare.

CHAPTER TWENTY

RAVEN

WE FELL INTO A FAMILIAR routine now that this side of the prison was better developed. Breakfast in our cells, occasional flight exercises through a wired-in section of the yard, optional gym time, and dinner if we were lucky. Even the cullings had been eliminated for the time being, the last one having wiped out half of the inmates transported to this side of the prison. New recruits were starting to show up again, so I imagined there would be another challenge soon.

Recon had been scarce to none, unfortunately. We'd lain low for an entire month, and it felt like we'd learned nothing. The flight exercises kept a strict view of the sea, and anywhere else we went had only revealed more cliffs and walls. I had no idea where solitary might be, and Mousey Mouse traveled through crevices and tunnels that were useless when it came to actually mapping out the prison. We also hadn't seen him since the gym incident. I didn't want to think about what that meant for our little guy.

So, yeah, we weren't getting anywhere.

Every day kept me busy—paying attention to rumors, flying high enough to try to glimpse over the black rocks without getting clipped by the restrictive wiring, and working out in the gym—but it wasn't showing the fruit I'd hoped for.

At least after our little showdown with the Valkyries, the hierarchy seemed to be falling back into place with the inmates giving me and my mates a wide berth. Sure, sometimes a male tried to cop a feel, but only if he wanted to lose a hand.

I didn't let myself fall into a false sense of security, though. Bryn, the last remaining Valkyrie, was definitely going to try something. It was only a matter of when.

I felt her eyes on me as I practiced a set at the gym, working against a wooden dummy in a flurry of punches Sorin had taught me. When I ventured a peek, she grinned and began sparring against one of her unfortunate volunteers.

As always, I watched with a mixture of disgust and fascination. The deal was that if a male could beat her, she'd fuck him. If he couldn't? Well, he wouldn't live to worry about it.

No one had survived her challenge so far, but there was no lack of sparring partners for the gorgeous Valkyrie with emerald eyes and lustrous black hair. She launched against her latest opponent, moving even faster than I was able to as she expertly adjusted her wings just enough to give her a thrust into the air before clamping them hard against her back, reducing her drag.

The male didn't bother trying to dodge and instead braced his escrima stick for the blow. She smashed straight into it, sending splinters flying everywhere, demonstrating both speed and strength in her attack—a benefit of being a warrior female.

"I think this'll be a record," remarked Zian as Bryn moved in for the kill.

"Nah, the one three days ago lasted less than ten

seconds," Sorin replied. "I think he actually fell *into* her dagger."

"Bitch and a cheat," I cursed, making both my Noir grin. They loved it when I was ticked off.

But it was so annoying. When I imagined a warrior, I thought of Sorin, who would always win in a fair fight, or even honorably lose when he believed it was the right thing to do, like when he saved my life.

This creature held no honor, and she proved that point when she slipped a contraband dagger from her leather straps and cut a long gash across her opponent's throat.

Blood sprayed over her, and she immediately turned to grin at me. She ran her blade across her neck in a taunting motion to suggest that I would be next.

"I can't believe the guards let her keep that thing," Zian said mournfully.

One glance at the cameras that dutifully watched us said the guards enjoyed the show far too much to take away Bryn's fun. Even if her power over the prison had diminished with the death of her two comrades, she was still a force to be reckoned with.

A deadly one.

I opened my mouth to suggest challenging her right here, right now, and hope that the guards would be entertained by it, but a strange sense of warmth ran through my body as if my healing magic had activated without warning.

A quick scan of my fingers and toes and then a glance down at the rest of my body indicated I was intact and unharmed. Nothing to explain the odd sensation.

"Did you feel that?" Sorin asked, straightening.

Huh. Not just me, then.

None of the other inmates reacted, but the Valkyrie broke her gaze from me as she scanned the room, her green eyes evaluating.

Something's up.

A slight tremble ran through the gym and was so subtle that I might not have noticed it had I not been on full alert. I felt the sensation in my feet first, since I preferred to go barefoot, and I called out a warning just in time.

"Get off the floor!" I shouted as I launched into the air.

Zian and Sorin obeyed me without question, following me with a hard thrust of their wings while we hovered, struggling against the still air as we reached the gym's ceiling.

"Rave, what is it—" Zian began, then the entire floor fell out in the back section where we'd been working out, replaced with molten lava that burst heat into the air and made an instant sheen of sweat break out over my whole body.

I stared, unable to believe what I was looking at.

"What the fuck?!" I shrieked as I beat my wings and tried to get closer to the ceiling to escape the burst of heat. If this was a culling, they were doing a good job of keeping us on our toes, quite literally.

Unfortunately, not everyone had paid attention to my warning. Noir who hadn't been fast enough screamed in agony as their wings caught fire. They sank into the molten flow overtaking the back portion of the gym, while the survivors had either launched into the air like us or were struggling to get to the single exit.

One where Bryn was already at the lead.

She grinned at me, then blew a kiss as she flapped her wings and beat everyone outside, only to slam the door closed and flip the dead bolt.

"Bitch!" I screeched.

Inmates beat at the door, but it was too late.

We were trapped.

The lava flow spread throughout the entire gym within a matter of minutes, forcing the rest of the Noir into the air.

"I can't keep this up," I said, panting as I fought to stay aloft. We didn't do near enough flight training to build the muscles necessary for hovering in stagnant air. I caught the few waves of heat that helped me hover, but it wasn't a sustainable plan.

"Look there," Sorin said, his finger pointing to a corner of the gym I might have missed in my panic. Lava worked at a foundation column and sent a crack up its spine. "If we break that, this portion of the compound might come down."

"Brilliant plan," Zian chided. "Being boiled by molten lava isn't enough for you. You want us to get buried alive, too?"

"Not if we break it at the right angle," I said, spotting the weaknesses of the structure that the others might not be able to see. "Follow my lead."

I wasn't strong enough to deal the damage necessary to take out the column, but I rammed it with my shoulder anyway, grunting with pain before fluttering off as Zian and Sorin went next. It took them three strong hits before another crack formed. "One more!" I shouted, backing out of the way in preparation for the ceiling to come down.

Sorin rammed the column, sending rocks of the collapse careening into the lava below. "To your left!" I shouted, and Sorin obeyed my instruction immediately, narrowly escaping the crash of debris that fell in his wake.

Sunlight poured in, and elation replaced my rising panic. I burst through the opening, gulping in fresh air from outside, but halted once I hit the perimeter. I cursed. "Damn it!"

Zian chuckled as he and Sorin followed me. They weren't stupid enough to fly any farther than I had, and we watched with mild irritation as one of the Noir zoomed past us and fried himself on the barrier.

We couldn't escape the prison, but at least we were still alive.

For now.

CHAPTER TWENTY-ONE

ZIAN

ACROSS THE YARD, Bryn preened, her wings fanning outward in a queenly manner that had me contemplating how quickly I could heft one of these charcoaled rocks through her black heart.

She had absolutely no regrets about locking us all in the gym yesterday, and it showed on her glowing face.

Raven stood beside me, her expression equally furious. "That bitch needs to die."

"Agreed," I muttered, folding my arms.

Sorin joined us on my other side, his wing brushing mine. "I'd say we should take her out now, but the Nora are up to something." He nodded toward the cliff, piquing my interest. It was his turn to perform surveillance today while I worked with Raven.

However, we'd cut our sparring short when Bryn sauntered into the courtyard in all her Valkyrie glory.

Just because she couldn't lock us out here didn't mean

167

she couldn't come up with something else just as deadly. I didn't want to be anywhere near that conniving cunt.

"Come have a look," Sorin encouraged, his intrigue palpable.

I followed him to the electrical edge, where energy hummed ominously through the air, and followed his gaze to the flurry of white feathers in the distance. Sorin stood with his feet braced, arms crossed, the stance expertly defensive.

And I immediately understood why.

"They're building something," I said, narrowing my gaze. "Another prison?"

"Maybe." He sounded perplexed yet curious.

I shared that feeling, the sensation only increasing as I caught sight of a pair of notorious black-tipped white wings. "Sayir's here," I breathed, shock rolling through my system.

"Yeah." Sorin's easy reply told me he'd already noticed the distinctly colored wings. No one else in the Nora kingdom had white feathers tipped with black. The rumor was, it'd happened when Sayir accepted his role as the Reformer. His brother, on the other hand, had white wings rimmed in gold, denoting him as the Nora King.

When I explained that out loud to a gaping Raven, her lips parted. "So that's him? The one all the Noir females warned me about?"

"What were their warnings?" I wondered out loud, genuinely curious. Sayir wasn't all that terrifying, just a royal-blood angel with a chip on his shoulder. Sort of expected, given his position and responsibility for the Noir.

"They called him wicked and cruel and said that when he takes females, he keeps them for nefarious purposes like breeding." She shivered, her fear of him tangible in the air.

I shared a glance with Sorin, who seemed as confused as I was. "The females at your former penitentiary spoke from experience?" he questioned.

She shook her head. "More like rumors created after other Noir disappeared."

"Noir like you?" I suggested, arching a brow. "Will they

assume he took you?"

She lifted a shoulder. "Probably not. Everyone always expected me to be moved to an adult prison once I turned eighteen. I grew up knowing that would be my fate and wasn't surprised at all when the Nora guard showed up on my birthday to escort me to the transport. It'd been more of a shock to find it full of male Noir. Fortunately, they couldn't see me because of the hoods."

"Did they drop you in the air?" Sorin asked. "Because I found you flying solo."

She licked her lips, her eyes gleaming with pride. "I stabbed the guard who was trying to fondle me and escaped the transport."

My eyebrows shot up. "And they didn't punish you for it?"

She shook her head. "No. They probably figured the arena was punishment enough."

My gaze returned to Sorin, who gave me a look that probably rivaled my own. "I'm surprised they didn't whip you or break a wing before the arena," he muttered. "It's what they would have done to us if we'd done something like that."

"Maybe they let it slide because she's a female?" I suggested, not sure I believed that excuse but coming up empty regarding other reasons as to why they'd allow her behavior.

"The one guard did say they weren't supposed to touch me, but then he seemed to be looking the other way."

"Then maybe they were worried about reprimand from a superior if they reported it." A plausible enough explanation, though it seemed to be lacking.

Sorin's expression told me he felt the same, but he didn't comment on it.

Yet another mystery for our list.

With that thing out in the ocean rising to the very top. "If that's our new home, it's small," I mused, comparing the castle-like compound behind us to the speck out at sea. It rivaled the size of our courtyard, which was a lot larger than our last one, but it was not big enough to hold challenges, a gym, and the dozens of cells inside.

"Whatever it is, I think we'll be introduced to it soon." Sorin studied it a moment longer before taking in the area around us once more, his blue eyes ever vigilant. "How are we going to kill Bryn?"

"Violently," Raven replied immediately. "Preferably with fire because I want to hear her scream."

I chuckled. "My, what a vicious little creature you've turned out to be, sweet bird."

She bared her teeth at me. "You have no idea."

"Oh, I think I have a very good idea," I countered, wrapping my palm around her nape to tug her up against me. "And I take a lot of credit for it, too."

Sorin snorted. "Yeah, you've done all the hard work."

I grinned at him. "It's been a joint project."

Raven rolled her eyes. "You act like I was this tiny, docile Noir before we met."

"You were," I insisted. "A sweet, innocent, darling little angel begging to be taken by two big Noir males."

Her pupils flared, her wings ruffling in the incoming breeze. "A feisty and fierce female with quick movements and a sharp intellect," she countered. "With a hint of innocence."

Sorin chuckled this time. "Sure, little dove. We'll go with that."

She growled. "I wasn't weak."

"We never said you were," I replied, leaning in to give her a kiss meant to soothe the angry lines forming around her mouth. "You're exceptionally strong, Raven. We know that. And you continue to grow more powerful every day."

"Making you the perfect mate," Sorin added, his fingers playing over her wings. "We would never allow a weak female in our bed, Raven. Not unless we wanted to risk breaking her."

"And we never feared breaking you," I whispered, drawing my tongue across her lower lip. "You're ours for a reason, sweet bird."

I allowed myself a moment to indulge in her kiss, loving the way her body melted into mine. Then I drew back when

I sensed the eyes of others on us. Everyone knew we'd mated, could scent the mingling of our pheromones in the air. Many of the males watched us with interest, envy evident in their gazes.

Meanwhile, Bryn glared at us with murderous intent.

She'd wanted us to perish in the gymnasium yesterday. That desire marked her as a coward. A true warrior took out his or her opponents in proper combat, not by using other convenient means.

Raven would never stoop to that level.

She'd wait until a challenge arose.

Just like me and Sorin.

It was why the three of us were the ideal triad. We understood each other in a manner no one else would. Not even Novak, really. He'd be able to relate on some levels, but never the one that tied us intimately. Because he'd never be part of this bond.

Although, that didn't lessen my connection to my cousin.

I could feel him pacing, waiting for the right moment. He'd lessened the block between us, allowing me to glimpse his emotions once more. It told me whatever perceived threat he'd faced was no longer around.

But the Warden had yet to release him from solitary.

Soon, I felt his aura telling me. A soft stroke of anticipation. *I'll be there soon.*

"Novak is ready to rejoin us," I said, pulling away from Raven to focus on Sorin. "I can sense his expectation to be released."

"Because Sayir is here?" Sorin asked.

I lifted a shoulder. "Maybe. I'm not sure." I studied the Nora in the distance again, my lips flattening. "But something is coming. I can feel it on the wind."

Sorin nodded. "Me, too."

"Any idea what?" Raven asked, her hands glued to my abdomen as she faced me instead of the water.

I brushed a stray strand of her dark hair away from her gorgeous face. "No. But whatever it is, it won't be good. We need to be prepared. And Bryn needs to die."

On that, we all agreed.

CHAPTER TWENTY-TWO

SORIN

A MAZE.

The structure formed over the last several weeks, Sayir's notorious black-tipped wings a constant ornament on the wind.

"What's he up to now?" I wondered out loud while we watched him fly in circles around the new creation. Several of the Noir observed along with us, everyone wearing the same expressions of dread as we stood along the cliff's edge of the courtyard. A light hum in the air warned us of the electric currents running a few feet away from our noses, but no one seemed bothered by it. We were all too enthralled by the new labyrinth glowing out in the sea.

The Reformer was not well liked among us, his reputation for cruelty renowned. He was charged with rehabilitating an entire race of miscreants—or that seemed to be his outlook, anyway—and so far, he'd failed. That had to burn a little, maybe even made him desperate. But this reformatory was not the solution.

Sometimes I wondered if a Noir could ever actually become a Nora again or if we remained forever Fallen.

However, the thing I never understood was how one infraction could earn a Noir an eternity of imprisonment. Yes, Zian and I had chosen to follow Novak's instincts over our orders. Yet we were trapped in prisons with murderers. Who decided our crimes were equal? And why?

"Something's about to happen," Zian murmured, somewhat replying to my question about Sayir's antics. "He's close to a major reveal."

"Of his maze?" Raven asked.

Zian nodded. "Looks more like a death trap to me."

"Another challenge," I added. "I wonder if we'll be dropped inside it and told to survive."

"Sounds just like this hellhole." Zian folded his arms, his eyes narrowing. "No, this is something else. He's taking too much time with it just to release us all and watch us survive. But what does it have to do with reform? Looks more like a warrior track to me."

Yeah, that was my thought, too. "It reminds me of fledgling training."

"Exactly." He scratched his chin, his dark hair sticking out at all ends, as usual. "Whatever he's up to, we'll know soon."

"So we need to be prepared," Raven translated.

We both nodded. "Yeah. We'll start by—"

"Breeder," one of the Nora guards snapped, interrupting me in midsentence. "You've been summoned."

"By who?" I demanded, shifting to stand in front of her.

She threaded her fingers into my plumes, giving them a tug. "Don't," she whispered. "I can handle myself."

I knew that, but something about this felt off.

Fuck, everything about this place itched at my nerves. More so today than any other day and I couldn't figure out why.

It was that maze.

Or maybe Sayir's involvement.

Why hadn't he made himself known to the inmates? Why was he hovering at sea? What had him so intrigued over there?

Zian grabbed my arm, tugging me slightly to move out of Raven's way when I didn't immediately shift. "She needs us at full strength," he muttered under his breath. "Don't make a scene."

Too late, I thought, catching the fury radiating from the Nora guard.

"The Reformer needs a test rat. He requested her." His smile was cruel. "I suppose I can give you a moment to say goodbye. Of course, you'll feel her die soon enough."

Raven froze.

And Zian reacted, his fist hitting the jaw of the Nora with a speed I would have admired if I wasn't well on my way to fight him myself.

So much for not making a scene, I thought as I slammed my heel into the guard's groin.

A burning sensation met my flesh as two Nora guards appeared out of nowhere, their weapons striking me repeatedly in an effort to bring me to the ground.

I turned around in a blind fury, knocking them out, ripping feathers from their spines by the fistful while Zian fought beside me.

Then a net of electricity fell over my wings, bringing me to the ground beneath a wave of Raven's screams. I cringed, watching her flailing in the air with her feet kicking outward as two guards dragged her out of the courtyard while all the other Noir watched with frightened expressions.

None of them helped.

Not that I expected them to, but in that moment, I wanted to slaughter them all. Including the Nora guards kicking me repeatedly while the electricity thrummed through my veins. They must have worn boots that were immune, because *fuck,* they were putting a lot of force into those hits.

Zian growled somewhere nearby, his own fight still raging as we fought futilely to reach our Raven.

Until an avalanche of power fell upon us, the Reformer

landing in a furious flutter of feathers. "Release them," he demanded, snapping at the guards. "Unless you want to add two more Noir deaths to your records."

Apparently, Noir deaths are considered bad when not ordained as a challenge. Who knew?

The burning sensation lessened as the nets fell, but I remained on my knees beneath Sayir's control. He was a royal blood, a commander, with unique abilities to inflict his desire on a crowd. In this case, he required submission, so everyone around him gave it.

Including me and Zian, the persuasion overpowering our need to protect, but just barely.

"You'll watch from the podium. I'll even allow you to use your mating bond to help guide her. But she is my chosen test subject, and I will use her as I see fit." The words were nonnegotiable and earned a snarl from Zian.

I remained silent.

He'd given us permission to help her.

I'd rather accept that than be sent to solitary for trying to save her from a fate neither of us could control. We'd spent the last few weeks memorizing every nook and cranny of that maze. If we were allowed to observe her from above, we could easily guide her. She'd survive.

Just as Zian had said, she needed us at full strength.

So I conceded, my head in a bow, accepting Sayir's terms, while vowing retribution should I ever find myself outside of this horrifying place.

Zian must have arrived at the same conclusion, because he fell quiet.

"Where's Novak?" Sayir asked. I suspected he was scanning the crowd, but I didn't dare lift my head to check.

"Solitary, sir," I replied, tacking on the designation out of a respect I didn't quite feel. Yet it came naturally from a lifetime of devoting myself to the service. Odd how a century of incarceration hadn't absolved me of that habit.

"Solitary?" he repeated. "Why the fuck is he in solitary?"

"He killed the majority of the Noir in the arena," a guard replied. "We didn't want him taking out all the subjects in the prison, so we put him in solitary. Sir."

I smirked. *Fair.* Novak had a way of doing things that didn't always marry up to outside expectations.

"You mean all the subjects who have been killed anyway due to the Warden's inept supervision?" Sayir sounded part amused, part annoyed. "Fix it. And get these two up on the podium without killing them."

The energy lessened on my feathers, Sayir's presence dissipating as he left the yard in a thrust of his wings, slicing right through the electric barrier with ease. Either he wore something that shielded him from the charge or his power protected him.

I suspected the former but wanted to investigate the latter.

"You heard him," a Nora guard barked, yanking me upward with a cruel jolt on my arm. The blossoming bruises around his left eye told me why.

"Put some ice on it," I suggested casually. "Might help, but I can't offer advice for the rest of your face. That's a result of your mother, I'm afraid."

He shoved me to the ground, his fist about to meet my face as a wave of power blocked him from touching me.

"*Now!*" a voice shouted from the sky, Sayir still observing.

I smirked as the Nora guard cursed. "Just wait until he leaves," the guard threatened.

"Sure," I replied, jumping back to my feet before the guard could reach for me again.

Zian flashed me a look that said, *Stop dicking around.*

The pang of fear in our bonds forced me to comply.

Raven was in trouble and she needed our help.

We're here, I tried to tell her, sending warmth through the connection. *We're right here.*

CHAPTER TWENTY-THREE

RAVEN

PANIC RAN TINGLING SENSATIONS down my fingertips, and I curled them into fists, hoping the angel at my side couldn't see my fear. He'd appeared moments ago, no introduction required.

The Reformer.

And I was to be his *test rat*.

I wanted to believe I could survive anything this place threw at me, but a fucking labyrinth full of death traps? Even I had my limits.

Waves crashed against the rocky exterior and its winding cliffs. We stood atop the courtyard with a perfect view into the maze. I tried to commit the path to the exit to memory, but even from here, my eye wandered into dead ends.

Traps waited behind walls, and segments of it shifted, showing me that the maze would be ever changing, even if I did manage to memorize a path. To add insult to injury, they'd dropped creatures into it the other day who now prowled inside, putting the finishing touches on a new game I was not looking forward to playing.

"Isn't it glorious?" Sayir asked, finally speaking. I repressed a shiver that ran up my spine when he rested a cold hand on my small shoulder.

Why me? I wanted to ask. *Why are you here? How is this about reform?*

I bit my lip, holding in the questions, and refused to meet his dark gaze. I'd caught a glimpse of the black irises earlier, noted his lack of a soul within, and assumed his heart was just as dark.

A test rat, I repeated to myself. *Fuck you.*

A ripple of warning filtered through my bond, and I looked down at the courtyard as I searched for my lovers. I found them being restrained by five guards each—because that was how many it took to keep them away from me right now. I widened my eyes in a silent plea for them not to interfere. They'd already tried and failed.

I couldn't do this if they were hurt.

I needed my focus.

A ruffle of black-tipped wings caught my attention, and I realized the angel beside me was waiting for a response.

"Why am I here?" I asked, hating how small my voice sounded.

I glanced at Bryn on his opposite side, saw the excitement gleaming in her green orbs. She'd probably volunteered for this madness, maybe even suggested me as her counterpart. This was like a Valkyrie's wet dream. Death, destruction, and mayhem all in one place? She wouldn't have had to be asked twice to enter the challenge. This was a place she'd dive into headfirst.

Sayir patted my head like I was a pet, then gave one of my wings an appreciative stroke. The gesture seemed almost fatherly, and it creeped me the fuck out. "I've been watching the two of you, and I must say, you both have your strengths and weaknesses. I'm curious as to who's going to come out on top."

That was definitely not an answer.

Of course, I hadn't really responded to his inquiry

either.

This place is not glorious, I thought, recalling his question. *It's grotesque and wrong.*

Bryn flared her wings, allowing the wind to ripple through them as if she wanted to fly to the island right now.

I would have thought allowing us up on this cliff was a show of trust had I not seen the boats with aerial-specific guns. If we tried anything funny, we'd be shot right out of the sky.

Bryn gave me a once-over. "It's almost embarrassing to pit me against this breeder. But the maze, oh, I do approve." She flashed a toothy grin. "I wonder how you'll die. Maybe a monster will eat you in the first dead end you run into. Or perhaps you'll be impaled by the moving spikes." Her tongue flashed out to wet her blood-red lips as her green eyes locked on me. "If you survive long enough, then I'll be the one to end you. Oh, how fun will that be?"

The Reformer gave Bryn the same appreciative stroke down one wing. The pride in his gaze utterly confused me. Were they related? Or did he treat all females this way?

There were rumors at the all-female penitentiary that he sometimes took angels and never returned them. No one knew what he did to them, but as they were usually women who disappeared, certain assumptions arose as a result.

I really didn't want to be one of his new toys, or whatever he called his female Noir.

Sayir captured my gaze, his expression almost kind. "I chose you, Raven," he started, his voice soft as he referred to my earlier question, "because I want to test the quality of my new maze. And who better to help me with that task than my two daughters?"

Every muscle in my body went taut, my mouth going dry.

Daughters?

"You're both equipped with the skills to survive. The question becomes, who will survive it better and come out on top?" he mused, his voice genuine in a way that made me sick to my stomach. "I suspect you'll both make me proud, but there's only room for one of you at Noir Reformatory. So may the best progeny win."

I gaped at him and then at Bryn, who widened her grin in response. Her hatred became so much clearer to me now.

She knew.

She knew this entire fucking time that we were not just sisters but also this bastard's offspring.

How could she not say something?

How did I not know?

Did any of the females who raised me know? Was one of them actually my mother? No. No, that wasn't possible. Someone would have told me.

I'm the Reformer's daughter?

This had to be a dream. A nightmare. Make-believe. This couldn't fucking be happening.

But his expression remained so fond and endearing, like a father doting on his children. Except this monster gave us a lethal maze to play in rather than a normal gift.

My entire life was created for this moment, I realized in stark horror. *And no one told me.*

Yet Bryn had been given every detail. I could see it now in her eyes as she beamed with excitement.

I was set up to fail.

Unprepared. Alone. Without any parental guidance. While she had it all, marking her as the clear victor.

I have no chance.

And her smile said she knew it, too. "Best of luck, sister," she sneered.

* * *

WE WERE PERMITTED a short flight to the entrance of the maze. I felt a hundred guns tracking my every wingbeat, so I didn't dare think about flying anywhere other than where instructed.

Not that I would leave Sorin or Zian behind. That wasn't an option.

Bryn grinned at me as we flew in tandem, then launched herself with a burst of speed toward the maze's entrance. I was in no hurry to enter the horrid place. She wanted to activate some of the traps for me? Be my guest.

I spotted her when she landed, and she ran full force into a tunnel, going through the center path, arcing left and right and coming upon one of the monsters as if on purpose.

What's she up to?

I didn't have long to ponder it as I inevitably landed in the entrance corridor myself, looking up to see a force field shimmer over my head.

There would be no flying out of this maze.

Swallowing the hard lump in my throat, I faced three possible routes. I remembered them from when I'd studied the maze from the cliff. Two of the routes would grant further access to the maze, whereas the third would lead to a deadly trap.

Bryn had gone down the middle path, and the one on the right led to a room of spikes that closed in on the victim, if memory served, so that left me only one viable choice. I didn't want to run into the Valkyrie if I could help it. She had brutal plans for me, and I had no intention of helping her carry them out.

My sister.

I tried to process the thought, but it stuck in my head like a thorn. There was no way that crazy bitch was my sister. Yet I felt the truth of it in my veins.

The Reformer is my father.

That terrified me even more than my relation to the crazy bitch. I looked up, longing for Sorin or Zian to assure me I wasn't evil. To tell me I wasn't anything like the madman who ran this place and made our lives a living hell on a daily basis.

As if in response to my plea, a shimmering gold-and-blue haze formed, guiding a path down the center corridor where Bryn had gone.

I paused, sniffing the air and scenting salty caramel that inexplicably reminded me of my mates, but why would they tell me to follow Bryn?

It has to be a trap. They can't help me here.

Deciding not to trust it, I took the left path.

My father likely had been encouraging my courtship so that he could study it, or worse. Perhaps he could re-create the pheromones that mixed when we were all together. It occurred to me then with a sickening thought why I had been allowed to mate. I was just another experiment to him. I had been born with black wings, meaning my progeny might carry the same trait.

If I survived, would he expect me to produce more of my kind?

Fierce protectiveness made my wings flare. I would have fledglings with Sorin and Zian one day, and if anyone tried to lay a hand on them, I would rip their throats out with my teeth.

A whirring sound caught my attention, and I shrank my wings close to my back. I remembered the feather-shearing devices I'd witnessed the other day. The angels had struggled to install it, the trap designed to clip necessary primary feathers.

Not a friendly adaptation to implement when the being in charge of the installation has wings.

I spotted one of the machines on the wall, running around a track I might have missed had I not known to look for it. The long, horizontal mark showed me the path the instrument would run through, which made it seem like a poor trap. Surely I could avoid—

A flash of metal made me yelp as I ducked just in time to miss one of the apparatuses whirring past at an insane speed. A long, nearly invisible arm swung out, cutting through the air and clipping the tip of my hair, sending black strands floating to the ground.

That was close.

Okay, so maybe my view from the cliff had left much to be desired in terms of reconnaissance. It was a fair distance away, after all.

The cackle of a crazed Valkyrie sounded through the corridor, and a monstrous screech followed. I couldn't decide who was winning, but I was glad I was nowhere near Bryn and whatever nightmare roamed her section of the maze.

Catching my breath, I continued down the narrowing path until I had no choice but to crawl. I considered going back, but if I could avoid my sister and reach the end of this maze, then I wouldn't have to kill her. I hoped some trap or creature would maim her first, because sororicide was a sin I really didn't want to add to my list.

My healing magic activated as my knees scraped against the unforgiving ground while I continued to crawl across the jagged rocks. The entire maze seemed to be made of the same black sheets of the cliffs—sharp and merciless.

I left a trail of blood in my wake as a result—a path my sister could follow if she decided to backtrack—but there wasn't much I could do about it.

Sweat ran down my neck by the time I spotted a glimmer of light at the end of the tunnel. Slowing down, I squeezed through the opening and into yet another room with multiple paths. I brushed myself off as I considered them. I squinted as I attempted to coax my memory into cooperating and held up my fingers to try to visualize.

"Okay, so, I went left, then there was a tunnel, and now I'm in a large room. When I was on the cliff, I saw, uh, I saw a blob that connected to other blobs."

I sighed. Yeah, this wasn't going to end well.

That golden-blue haze returned again, this time flashing down a corridor to my far right as if panicked.

What's it trying to tell me now?

A snap nearby was my only warning, and I flared my wings, bolting out of the way just in time as an enormous fireball zoomed right through the place I'd been standing. I gulped in fresh breaths of air as my adrenaline kicked in, and another series of clicks sounded.

There was no time to try to remember which way to go or to decide if the magical haze that smelled like my mates was trustworthy. I had to pick a path, and I had to pick one now.

Praying to all the gods I didn't believe in, I opted to follow my gut, and I took the middle path at full speed just as another series of fireballs sent the entire room up in flames. I kept my eyes peeled for any signs of new traps or danger and sucked in air when the room opened up to the sea.

I skidded to a halt.

This is one of the blobs I saw from the cliff, I realized.

I scanned the expanse before considering the best way across. Tiny wires shimmered throughout the space, promising that any attempt at flight over the choppy waves would result in being sliced into itty-bitty pieces.

Looking back, the golden-blue haze flitted around me, sending kisses and warmth over my body before disappearing off the cliff and into the water.

Now it wants me to swim?

My gaze fell to the dark waters, and I shivered. I'd never tried swimming before, not that I'd ever had a chance.

I ruffled my wings as I considered whether I could even handle being underwater and glanced up at the sky. Sayir—I refused to think of him as my father—was probably enjoying the show at my expense. Just the notion incited anger in me, making me hate him even more.

"You think this is funny, prick?" I muttered, balling my fists as rage burned through my system.

A screech from behind me cut me off, and I peeked over a wing to see one of the nightmarish ink blobs hauling ass with a dagger sticking out of its eye.

Damn Valkyrie had somehow managed to piss it off and then sent it after me!

My prayers turned to curses as I clutched my wings to my back and pointed my fingers, diving into the water without a second thought.

Cold rushed over me with biting fangs and took my breath away. Water penetrated my wings and immediately caused me to start sinking. Goose bumps fled down my limbs as my stomach clenched.

I flung my wings outward on instinct, praying my reaction was right.

It was.

The force kicked me upward, and I burst through the surface long enough to suck in a gulp of air before I sank again.

Thrust. Kick. Gulp. Repeat.

I went on like that for what felt like forever, and fatigue threatened to make me give up, but I sensed Sorin and Zian waiting for me at the other end of my mate-bond. I couldn't let them down now, not when they were counting on me to survive.

If you die, we die, they seemed to be telling me. *And we're not dying today. So move your ass!*

My hands hit jagged rocks on the other side, and I clutched onto them, my healing magic working in overdrive as it tried to keep up with my lack of oxygen and the cuts that sprang across my flesh while I scrambled up the uneven wall.

I allowed myself a moment of reprieve as I collapsed on the other side, drenched, freezing, and exhausted.

"Well, don't you look like a little drowned rat," sneered a female voice, making every muscle in my body tense up.

Bryn.

"I don't want to fight you," I said through chattering teeth as I tried to stand up and failed, unaccustomed to the massive weights on my back.

She stepped on one waterlogged wing, making me cry out as she twisted her foot.

"That's a shame, because it's all I've thought about since I got here." She leaned in and tapped a plump lip. "Now, how should I kill you? Slowly, obviously. Maybe I should rip off your wings, first?" She patted down her leather garb and clicked her tongue, still keeping my wing pinned with her foot. "Right, I used the dagger Dad gave me on my new pet." She straightened, released my wing, and whistled. I glanced behind me as the ink creature screeched, then it disappeared into the tunnel. "It'll be here shortly. The path I took swings around this ocean trap. Looks like you're not as smart as you think you are."

Huh, maybe I should have listened to the golden-blue magic cloud.

"Honestly, I thought your yummy mates had taught you better than this." She leaned in again, taunting me with her proximity, her overconfidence toxic. "When you're gone, they're going to beg me for sex and I'm going to indulge them. Hell, I might not even kill them right away. True warriors are hard to find, you know."

I screamed, knowing she was goading me, but I didn't care. Unlike me, she was as rotten on the inside as her black wings suggested.

Her wild green eyes lit up with delight when I unsteadily leapt up to my feet and swung a fist at her. She deflected it with ease, my exhaustion making the punch clumsy and slow. Yet I tried again for good measure because the bitch had pissed me off.

She dodged, using my momentum against me as I stumbled onto the ground once more, landing hard on another sheet of spiky shards. It split my skin, raking pain up my spine and blurring my vision with tiny black dots.

She clicked her tongue again—a habit I was beginning to hate.

"I killed Vivian," I reminded her. "She tried to take my mates from me, and look how that turned out for her."

Bryn had the audacity to throw her head back and laugh. "You really are as dumb as you look, *breeder*," she said, the last word with an added sneer. "I knew you'd win a fight if your mates were involved. The sexy one with the dark hair—Zian, right?—gave you a weapon. So you only won because of him. But guess what? You're all by yourself now. Nobody is here to save you this time."

A screech sounded through the corridors, warning us that the ink creature would be here soon. Bryn grabbed me by the hair and gave me a sharp yank, making me cry out as pain exploded over my scalp.

"I was hoping this would be a better challenge," she lamented, "but I came here to please Father. Torturing you will just be an added bonus."

A sense of hopelessness suffocated me inside, threatening my ability to fight back.

I'm screwed.

All of my training had capitalized on my speed, which was largely influenced by the use of my wings. Yet they were soaked through, making me slow and clumsy. Without

NOIR REFORMATORY: THE BEGINNING

my agility, Bryn was right. I wouldn't be a challenge at all.

Tears stung my eyes, and my heart twisted at the thought of what it would do to Zian and Sorin once they felt my death. I couldn't imagine hurting them in such a way, and a sob caught in my throat.

I felt their presence inside me, demanding me to focus, to not let her antics weigh me down. They still had faith in me, but I had no idea how or why. Couldn't they see my…?

Wait…

I canted my head, my gaze snagging on a faint black line dotting the wall with the tell-tale humming sound growing in the distance. Bryn hadn't spotted it, too focused on her *new pet* to notice.

That's it, I thought. *That's my chance.*

But I only had one shot at it.

Better make it count.

Waiting until the last possible moment, I lobbed another pathetic punch at Bryn, at which she laughed as she dodged out of the way…

And right into the path of the oncoming machine.

It sliced straight through her with ease, leaving a red trail through her midsection as her laugh cut short and her wide, green eyes locked onto me in shock.

Then her top half fell over as her knees crumpled to the ground, leaving her body in an unceremonious death.

A wave of nausea swept through me as I felt the weight of an unforgivable sin rest in my soul. I had a feeling that had I been born a Nora, this would be the moment my wings turned black. Only, I never had a choice. I was always this way, my fate chosen before my birth.

I staggered to my feet and rubbed my head, feeling dizzy, but the shrieking sounds of the monster said I didn't have time to collect myself.

I considered the multiple paths and felt another crushing wave of hopelessness weigh me down. It didn't matter that I had survived Bryn, because there was no way I could make it out of this damn place alive.

A niggling sensation in my mate-bond spurred to life until my chest felt like it would swell and explode.

Sorin.

Zian.

They were still watching me from the cliffs. I could sense their pride and determination, their urging for me to continue forward.

Don't give up.

Fight.

Run.

That glittering haze appeared again, a mixture of blue and gold that tickled my nose with the sweet scent of salty caramel. It bubbled to life, fluttering as if telling me to stop being stubborn, and swept down the far-left path.

"Thank you," I whispered as tears sprang to my eyes, finally believing that my mates were trying to help me. I took a moment to gaze up at the clouds where my mates were watching, helping me in a way no one would see coming.

This was what the Valkyries would never have. Why I would always be stronger than they could ever hope to be. No matter what Bryn had said, I would never be alone.

I ran through the maze, following my heart to return to Sorin, to Zian, and promised them I would never let them out of my sight ever again.

Chapter Twenty-Four

RAVEN

I FOLLOWED THE GLOWING trail of my mates' love to freedom, only to run straight into Sayir instead.

Not what I'd been hoping for, but at least it wasn't the ink monster.

Sayir fluttered his black-tipped white wings and gave me a slow, steady clap. "Bravo, Daughter. Bravo."

I exited the maze, and the wall slid shut behind me. Three Nora angels and three guards without wings closed in around us, readying shackles as two of them activated a portal. I glanced at it, evaluating where I might be sent, before returning my attention to the grinning angel.

"Those won't be necessary," he said to the guards. "She's not going anywhere."

Yet, I nearly added out loud. Because there was no way in hell I intended to stay here. Not now that I knew the truth.

"Honestly, I expected the Valkyrie to win," he admitted.

"But you have never failed to surprise me, my dear." He folded his wings to his back, content with the outcome, and turned to walk up a path that overlooked the maze.

My dear, I repeated, seething inside. *I am not your anything, you fucking prick.*

But it wouldn't be wise to say that out loud.

Instead, I followed him, feigning curiosity. Bryn's favor amongst the guards was clear now. They all knew she was the Reformer's daughter. She'd accepted that fate with a smile. If I, too, played that card, maybe I'd be afforded some favors, like weapons and more yard time. Then I could use those favors against these assholes and escape.

Sometimes it paid to play along.

From the top of the hill, I stopped beside Sayir and scanned the impossibly large labyrinth that could very well have been my gravesite today. I intentionally tried not to find Bryn's body, but Sayir pointed it out anyway.

"There she is, one of the most vicious Valkyries of all time, and you killed her with nothing but your wit. Absolutely brilliant, Daughter. I should have never underestimated you." He grinned as he sighed, scanning the rest of the labyrinth with a sense of pride.

I endured the long silence, not sure if he expected me to respond. The guy was clearly a psycho, and an arrogant prick. Pricks loved to hear themselves talk. It was only a matter of time before he provided me with something useful.

"I built this prison for an important reason, Raven. One that requires your help."

Like I would do anything to help this asshole. I didn't respond, but my fingers curled into fists and my body began to tremble with the need to run far away from this maniacal angel.

He grinned as if pleased with my anger. "Don't worry, darling. The only thing required of you for now is to survive." He chuckled. "Oh, and continue to entertain your mates."

And there it was.

Cold, hard proof that the Reformer wanted me to mate.

Wanted to see what kind of fledglings I could produce for his benefit.

Not. Fucking. Happening.

I would talk to Sorin and Zian about this. They had mentioned that when an angel went into heat, I'd know it, and it shouldn't be for years to come, but I was a Noir. Maybe I worked differently, and if we were still in this godforsaken hole in the ground when that time came, we needed to be prepared for it.

"I really had it all wrong," he continued, oblivious of my rising fury. "Brynhild's mother was a Valkyrie, and I thought that would make her stronger. Physically, it did. She was quite impressive, but nothing like you. She lacked the wit, the heart, and the incessant need for survival that makes you so special." He hummed, locking his arms over his chest. "Yes, I will definitely pursue breeding with more like your Nora mother. The outcome seems more viable."

"So that's what this is all about? Mating?" I guessed.

He glanced at me, his eyebrow inching upward. "No. This is about survival, Raven. Surely you understand that concept by now."

"But why?" I demanded. "Why all the tests? Why raise me with black wings? Why put me through this hell?"

"To strengthen you, my child. To ensure you survive what's to come. And to use your guidance with the others." He sounded prophetic, his age showing with each statement. This male lacked morals. He saw his own progeny as test subjects, not angels. He created a maze to test the Noir, to ensure only the strongest remained.

But I didn't understand why.

"What do you gain from all this?" I wondered out loud, my arms stretching wide to include his maze into the insanity of the question. "What's the point of surviving when hell is the reward?"

"Perhaps hell is only the temporary sacrifice. Perhaps another kingdom is the intended reward," he replied cryptically, his finger brushing my nose in a tender stroke that belied our conversation. "I've lived a thousand years in purgatory, Raven. I'm tired of purgatory. Together we shall inspire change."

My heart skipped a beat. "What kind of change?"

"The necessary kind," he replied, turning back toward the hill to begin his descent. "Bryn dreamed of the ideal challenge, with which I provided her. But your dream is of freedom. I can give you that, Raven. But I require your compliance in exchange for it. I need your leadership."

He wasn't making any sense.

"Leadership of what?"

He smiled. "You'll see, darling. And soon, too." He stopped just before the portal, his hands clasping together. "The key to everything just arrived, Raven. I think you'll like her. But she'll need your help to thrive here. Can you do that for me? Can you help guide her?"

I gaped at him. "I have no idea what or who you're talking about."

"Ah, but you will. And I think you'll do just as I requested, despite your dislike of me." His lips curled. "You have the heart of a Nora but the soul of a Noir. Listen to the latter. It'll serve you well."

The guards shoved me through the portal before I could reply.

And directly into my quarters.

Relief settled across my shoulders, the nest smelling like my mates, like home.

Until I realized Sorin and Zian weren't waiting for me inside, but a lethal angel with hair as dark as midnight was. The wicked gleam in his eyes betrayed a keen sense of intelligence, one that matched the flattening of his lips.

"Oh, uh, you must be Novak," I whispered.

He didn't reply.

Instead, he wrapped his palms around my throat and hoisted me up against the wall.

Fuck.

CHAPTER TWENTY-FIVE

ZIAN

Five Minutes Earlier…

MY FEATHERS FLEXED in the incoming night air, my gaze on that maze in the distance as Raven's panic shot through our bond. It killed me that I couldn't go to her, to soothe her. She was still too far away, her essence enmeshed in that damn death trap island in the middle of the fucking ocean.

"She won," Sorin said, his expression one of confusion. "I felt her victory."

"I know." *After she ignored us several times,* I thought, slightly irritated. She must not have understood what we were doing because it wasn't like her not to trust us.

"So why is she terrified?" Sorin asked.

I shook my head, unable to answer that. Because I had no clue what was happening. My only saving grace was being able to sense the fullness of her spirit. While she might be afraid, she wasn't hurt. And part of her was thriving on a wave of fury.

That knowledge meant everything right now.

Because without it, I'd be tempted to try my luck with the energy force field. And Sorin would be right beside me.

The guards had left us alone as soon as she'd escaped the maze. We thought they meant to bring her back to us, but it seemed they had other plans.

Where are you, Raven? Why are you scared?

Sorin and I continued to pace until a new shock of fear trickled through our connection, this one much closer.

I shared a glance with Sorin before we took off at a sprint for our cell, Raven's energy signature a beacon to our senses.

I reached the door first to find her pinned up against the wall with Novak's hands wrapped around her throat, his eyes narrowed as he sniffed her.

Sorin growled in warning, causing my cousin to slowly draw his gaze to where we stood in the doorway. He didn't release Raven, but I noticed his grip lessening in severity. His head tilted in an eerie manner I recognized, his mind working through the situation at rapid speed.

Then, in typical Novak fashion, he shrugged and let Raven go. His wings gave a little ruffle as he collapsed into our makeshift nest and closed his eyes.

That was it.

No hello.

No sentiment of missing us.

Just him evaluating our choice and deciding to accept it without a single fucking word.

Sorin grabbed Raven, yanking her into a crushing hug while I drew my fingers over her throat to ensure Novak hadn't damaged her. She shuddered, her feathers pulled tight to her back. I stroked her soft plumes, offering her comfort while Sorin gave it to her with his mouth, kissing her as if he thought he might never kiss her again.

Feeling as though we'd acquired an audience, I glanced down to find Novak watching the embrace with mild curiosity. "Are you seriously going to lie there and not say a damn word about being in solitary?" I demanded. "Or ask what we've been up to?"

"It's obvious what you two have been up to in my absence," he replied, his voice low, as if he hadn't used it in ages. Knowing him, he probably hadn't. "Congratulations."

And that was it.

His grand speech.

I wanted to pull him into a bear hug and throttle him at the same time.

Instead, I focused on Raven, kissing her the same way Sorin had while he ran his hands over her to check for any residual damage. But I knew through our bond that she was fine. Her terror had subsided now that we were together, and she broadcast a sense of calm that allowed my heart rate to slow for the first time in what felt like years.

"You did good," Sorin praised her, his hands on her face as he took her mouth away from mine. "You did so good, little dove," he repeated, kissing her again. "Apart from that first left turn through the fire, anyway."

The subtle hint of chastisement in his tone rivaled my thoughts. She'd blatantly ignored our suggestion and chose the worst route to take.

"Fire?" she repeated, her brow furrowing. "There was no fire."

Sorin and I shared a look before I slowly replied, "There was definitely fire lining that left path. We could feel it heating you up through the bond. We didn't understand why you picked that path."

"There wasn't any fire." She sounded certain, but we'd seen the flames curling around her from above.

"Similar to the challenge?" Sorin asked. "Like when we could see through the fiery perimeter and she couldn't?"

"That's not good," I muttered. "It implies they're playing with our vision or hers." And I suspected it was hers because we both could see her fight against Vivian during that challenge, while she'd been blinded to our fights.

"Yeah, it does," he agreed, frowning.

Raven shook her head. "We can figure that out later. I-I need to tell you something."

Novak closed his eyes, already bored apparently.

I ignored him in favor of Raven. "We know what happened in the maze, Rave. We felt every second of it. Including when you ignored our advice."

She shook her head. "Not that. But thank—"

"If you thank us for helping you survive, I'm going to fuck you against that wall while Novak watches," Sorin threatened, his anger palpable. "You're *our mate*, Raven. It's not a favor or us helping you when we ensure that you survive. You're connected to us. You die, we die."

I knew he meant that figuratively, not literally. Because, yeah, a part of us would be tormented for eternity without her, and we'd probably crave death. But we wouldn't actually perish if she did. Not physically. It would be our souls that suffered.

"What do you want to tell us, sweet bird," I interjected, taking her from Sorin's arms to wrap my hand around the back of her neck and hold her to me. "What happened after you completed the maze?"

"I met with the Reformer," she whispered with a shudder.

That seemed to intrigue Novak, because he sat up and drew his knees to his chest, his expression intense.

Sorin's wing brushed mine as we formed a protective wall around our Raven. "What did he say?" I asked her.

"I..." She swallowed. "He told me before... before the maze... He called me *daughter*."

The next several minutes while she recounted their conversations—there were *two*—were among some of the tensest moments of my life.

One could have heard a pin drop when she finished, all of us astounded by the information she'd just provided.

"Yeah, so, the Reformer is my father," Raven muttered, breaking the silence. "And the crazy bitch is my sister. Or was, anyway. She's dead now. I... I killed her."

Raven didn't appear saddened by the fact, just alarmed by the entire reveal. I understood because the news shocked me as well. "Did he say who your mother was?"

She shook her head. "Just commented on her being a

Nora. Bryn's mother was a Valkyrie. He's pleased with the outcome I've given him, so he's going to make more." She shivered, her arms going around herself. "And I think he might want…" She swallowed, trailing off.

"Might want what?" I asked softly, aware of her scurrying emotions. This had to be taking a toll on her. But my brave, sweet bird met my gaze, a hint of fire lurking in her dark irises.

"Our offspring."

"That'll never happen," Sorin replied immediately.

"Agreed." I'd kill the bastard before he touched our fledglings. But it did mean we would need to be careful whenever Raven went into heat. Fortunately, that shouldn't be for several years, if not a decade from now. And I didn't plan on us still being here when that happened.

"A key," Novak interjected from the floor, his focus clearly elsewhere. "Sounds about right."

He lay back down, his interest complete.

The three of us stared at him, waiting for more.

As usual, he remained quiet.

"Care to elaborate, Cous?" I asked him.

"No."

Of course not. "How about you do it anyway?" I told him, a demand underlining my tone. "The mouse told us about your demon friends that escaped."

Novak snorted as a squeak sounded in protest.

Raven spun around. "Mousey Mouse!" She hadn't seen the rodent since the gym incident and had feared something had happened to him. "Where are you?"

The little rodent peeked out of the blankets, climbing onto Novak's shoulder, and I took a step forward to warn my cousin not to harm that rodent, or he'd face a mighty pissed-off Sorin in response. Only, the thing pulsed with energy and began to shift into something more dragon-like than mouse-like, causing Raven to jump backward.

"Mousey Mouse?" she breathed as the thing finished its shift with a little puff of fire.

Novak lifted a hand to brush the resulting soot from his chest, his eyes still closed.

"What the fuck?" Sorin demanded.

"I can't hear him anymore," Raven said, frowning.

Novak sighed, his irritation evident. "Because he's mine. And he prefers the name Clyde."

My lips twitched. "You turned him into a mini-shifter."

His resulting grunt neither confirmed nor denied my comment. I shook my head, bemused. "Well, I never thought you'd be the type to entertain a pet, Cous."

Another shrug from the floor. He could have been napping, for all the emotions he showed on his face. Maybe he needed one after his time in solitary.

"Tell us what you think about the key," Sorin said, kicking at Novak's foot. "We're not all master strategists. Also, welcome back. We missed you. Thanks for being so enthusiastic about your return. And if you ever touch Raven again, I'll have your balls."

Novak's lip twitched at one side, the only sign of his amusement. "Sayir is up to something. I need some sleep. Then you'll tell me everything you've learned, and we'll develop a plan."

Wow, that was practically considered a speech in Novak Land.

He'd probably go silent for days now just to recharge.

Or maybe his months in solitary encouraged all those words.

"That's it?" Sorin asked, his brow furrowing. "You want a nap, then we'll talk about getting the fuck out of here?"

Novak remained silent, his affirmative answer hanging between us.

"How'd the demons do it?" I wondered out loud. "This place is a damn maze."

"Another realm, another game," Novak replied cryptically.

Meaning they were a different species living in an entirely different world of possibilities. "But surely some of what they did can help us, right?"

Novak scoffed. "Sayir's daughter will prove more valuable."

Raven bristled. "Don't call me that. I'm nothing like that

199

monster."

Novak shrugged as if to say, *Sure*. And went back to his nap.

Crazy fucker.

At least he'd spoken and answered some questions. That alone was a miracle.

"So we're going to find a way out of here," I said, mulling over everything he'd said in addition to Raven's conversation with Sayir.

Daughter. I'd say that gave us an advantage, but given what he did to his other daughter—Bryn—it seemed safe to assume he'd sacrifice Raven just as swiftly. Which meant we needed to strategize accordingly.

"And then we're going to figure out how to kill that asshole," Raven put in, her voice carrying a hint of vehemence that had been missing before. It seemed as though now that the shock of his information had dissipated, her need for revenge surged to the forefront of her thoughts. "My entire life has been an experiment. He's put me through hell just to see what I can handle. He even pitted me against my own sister simply to see who would come out on top."

Yeah, her ire was mounting by the second.

And it was a beautiful sight to behold.

"He won't get away with this. He can't. I refuse to let him. He's going to die."

"Excellent," Novak put in, approval radiating from that word alone.

She ignored him. "He's set up this entire reformatory as some giant experiment, and I want to know why because it's not about redemption."

Well, that much was true. "It's about death." Which certainly didn't equate to the Nora way, where one repented for their sins to earn back their white wings. Fighting other Noir to the death only seemed to darken our souls, not brighten them.

"I think it's about more than that," Raven replied, her expression intense. "His eyes gleamed with approval when I made it through the maze, like he was pleased to see his test subject pass his wicked test. And it had nothing to do with empowering my soul so much as ensuring my ability to fight for my life. He also claimed this place was about survival, implying that we need to be prepared for the future. That I need to help his supposed key, to lead. But to lead us all to what?"

"Warriors," Sorin whispered, his wings rustling with discontent. "He's training us to be warriors."

He was right.

That was why the maze had reminded us of our fledgling training days. Because the maze was *modeled* after them.

"But why?" I pondered out loud. "What need could he possibly have for an army?"

"A revolution." Raven's nostrils flared. "He's going to take on the Nora." She met my gaze, her own eyes wild. "It's the only reason that makes any sense."

"Except it doesn't because he's a Nora himself." Why would he go against his own kind?

"Is he?" she pressed. "Because his eyes are full-blown black, just like mine, and I swear his aura is just as dark. And how could a male charged with reform get away with treating the Noir this way? It doesn't make any sense."

"I've been saying that for decades," Sorin added, his brow furrowed. "The entire system is fucked up. And she's right. His soul has to be black for creating this place."

Raven nodded. "He's more wicked than all the creatures in here combined."

It all added up, but I didn't understand *how* he intended to see it through.

"If our assumptions are true, then we need to get the fuck out of here even more than we did before," Sorin muttered. "Because I refuse to be some pawn in a revolution, even if I want revenge for the Nora leaving us here to rot."

The grunt from the ground translated into an "I agree" from Novak. He'd already come to this conclusion himself, having seen all the angles well before us. Only, he hadn't given us the answers, forcing us to deduce the same theory from the details provided.

"Bastard," I muttered. He was lucky we had a family tie, or I'd throttle him.

His lips twitched again, this time on both sides. He appeared ready to say something when a commotion from the hallway had him sitting upright, his eyes opening in full alertness.

"Let go of me!" a female demanded. "I swear I didn't do anything wrong. I'm not supposed to be here."

"Your wings say otherwise, Princess," a male snapped. "Get the fuck in that cage or I'll toss you inside."

"That won't be necessary," a voice I recognized replied.

Novak and I shared a look as Sorin said, "Auric?"

The three of us darted into the hallway just in time to see the white-winged angel escorting a Noir with vibrant fuchsia hair into a cell with his grip on her elbow. She vibrated with agitation, her royal blood permeating the hallway with a lavish hint of rich jasmine and rose.

Auric turned to address the Nora guard, his bright blue eyes landing on us with a hint of surprise that quickly melted into disdain. "I'll handle her from here," he said in a low growl. "Touch her again and I'll kill you myself."

"Yes, sir," the Nora guard replied through his teeth before marching off down the hall.

"That female is the spitting image of Sefid's mate," Sorin whispered as Auric disappeared into the cell and slammed the door behind him.

Yeah, and she reeked of royalty.

"What the fuck is going on?" I asked, looking at a startled Raven before focusing on my cousin.

"I think the key Raven mentioned just arrived," Novak mused. "In the form of a Royal Princess with black wings." He stared at the door for a long moment. "Well, this should be fun. Looks like we'll be staying for a bit longer after all."

EPILOGUE

RAVEN

THE KEY TO EVERYTHING that the Reformer had referred to was the gorgeous Princess of the Nora.

She'll need your help to thrive here.

Can you do that for me?

Can you help guide her?

His words haunted me. If this chick really was the key to his plans, then I was more interested in killing her than helping her survive.

She'd been holed up in her cell for a week pretending to be feeble and scared. The fact that Sayir had assigned her a royal warrior said that she must be extra dangerous. I wasn't going to let my guard down.

"I hear that Layla convinced Auric to allow her outside today," Zian said with a sense of amusement. He nudged Novak, who watched the inmates with his perpetual sense of boredom. "What do you say, Novak? Curious to meet the princess?"

The deadly angel yawned.

"Poor Auric," Sorin said with a laugh. "I hear she's been giving him a hard time. You'd think he could handle such a little thing."

I rolled my eyes. "You have a penchant for underestimating females," I pointed out. "The last bitch Sayir sent here tried to kill me. I learned my lesson the first time."

"Someone sounds jealous," Sorin mused as he crossed his arms.

My lip curled in disgust. "Jealous? Please."

"I thought we told you that you were irreplaceable?" Zian ran a sensual touch down my spine between my feathers. He knew I loved it when he did that.

"I'm not jealous of her," I said. "I'm pissed that Say—" I cleared my throat, glancing at the inmates around us. They kept a reasonable distance from our infamous triad, and I had gained a modicum of respect since surviving the maze, but I lowered my voice anyway. "I'm pissed that the Reformer thinks he can just do whatever he wants. He brought his own niece to this hellhole, and she's spent the last week pretending like she doesn't belong here."

"And you think it's all for show?" Sorin asked, raising a brow. "She's the Princess of the Nora. I don't see what she could gain by intentionally Falling and getting herself locked up."

"Maybe," I begrudgingly admitted. "But she still did something bad enough to Fall, so if you want to underestimate her, fine. However, I'm not going to be fooled by a pretty face."

The guys fell into silence as they considered my train of thought. The Reformer had been one step ahead of us this entire time, and it felt like things were about to get much worse.

A murmur swept through the courtyard as the subject of our conversation stepped out onto the rocks. She wore elegant sandals that roped up her long legs, drawing the eye up her body, which was so perfect it almost hurt.

One of the inmates was stupid enough to approach her,

leering at her ample cleavage. "You finally came out to play, Princess."

"Just watch," I muttered to my mates. "You'll see. She's going to show her true colors."

I expected the princess to go all Valkyrie on the inmate's ass, and her royal warrior guard would be there to stop her. The inmate gave Auric, her ever-present personal guard, a lifted sneer. "Why don't you ditch the shiny toy and get yourself some real protectors? I could show you—" The Noir reached for her but didn't get to finish his sentence because Auric flashed out a blade, cutting off the inmate's hand.

The Noir shrieked in pain and fell to one knee as he grasped the amputated wrist that soaked the rocks with his blood.

"Anyone else want to lose a hand, or worse?" Auric shouted, his blue eyes dancing with danger as Layla went pale. The rest of the inmates backed away, giving the pair further space.

"Yeah, I see what you mean," Zian said sarcastically, earning a glare from me. "The princess is absolutely terrifying."

She shivered as fear clung to her. Her scent permeated the yard, royal in its likeness and obnoxiously pleasant with pungent jasmine and rose tones. She stepped around the bleeding angel and averted her gaze, looking instead to the sea with a sense of longing as she wrapped her arms around herself. Auric joined her with his hand on his weapon, his alert stance daring anyone else to approach.

Her words carried to me on the breeze. "I don't belong here," she whispered as she curled her wings protectively around herself.

Across from me, Novak rubbed at his nose, his boredom replaced by a dark intensity as he watched the princess. His fists opened and closed, and his wings vibrated.

I gave Zian a raised brow, curious as to what had irritated the savage angel.

He turned to his cousin and bumped his shoulder, the

two of them locking gazes for a long moment of understanding before Novak returned his focus to the fuchsia-haired female.

Oh... I'd seen that look before on Sorin's and Zian's faces.

Shortly after they'd met me.

Novak and the princess were compatible mates.

She fluttered her wings before glancing back, matching Novak's gaze with a flicker of fear mingled with interest.

Auric seemed to finally notice the two and slowly placed a hand low on her back, a move that seemed out of place for a guard. The intimate touch elicited a growl from Novak that I didn't think was entirely intentional.

Great. The key to Sayir's plans rested in the hands of a beautiful royal, and she was compatible with not only the deadliest Noir to ever exist but a royal Nora guard as well.

"It would be so much easier if I could just kill her," I whispered mournfully.

Novak finally broke his stare to lock onto me, his ice-blue eyes sparking with deadly rage. "I don't recommend it."

Four words underlined in lethal promise.

Right. Definitely a compatible mate.

Irritated, I ruffled my wings and crossed my arms, openly glaring at the princess, who had turned back to the sea. Her eyes were now locked on the labyrinth in the distance. While the cullings had been paused, Sayir still enjoyed dropping a handful of inmates who'd stepped out of line into the maze just to remind us all of our place.

The princess released a delicate gasp when one of the Noir succumbed to the spike trap. This was an unforgiving hellhole of a prison, and death was never far away.

Welcome to Noir Reformatory, Princess.

* * *

Noir Reformatory continues with *Noir Reformatory: First Offense*, featuring Layla, Auric, and Novak. Silence can be sexy...

Trapped in a world of sin and sexy alpha angels.
Forever defined by my black wings.

My father, King of the Nora, sent me to Noir Reformatory to
atone for crimes I didn't commit.

So what's a girl to do? Escape, obviously.

Except I need allies to accomplish that feat and no one wants
anything to do with King Sefid's daughter. If anything, my claim
to the throne has only made running that much harder, and
worse, I'm stuck with two hot angels standing in my way.

Auric is my supposed guardian, his white wings marking him as
my superior in this deadly playground. Only, I'm his princess
and I refuse to bow to a warrior like him.

And Novak, the notorious *Prison King*, is hell-bent on teaching
me my place. Which he seems to think is beneath him. In his
bed.

This prison resembles a training camp for soldiers more than a
reformatory for the Fallen. I suspect something nefarious is at
play here, but of course no one believes me. I'm the guilty
princess with black wings. Well, I'll prove them all wrong. I just
hope it isn't too late.

My Name is Princess Layla.
I'm innocent.
And I do not accept this fate.

ABOUT LEXI C. FOSS

USA Today Bestselling Author Lexi C. Foss loves to play in dark worlds, especially the ones that bite. She lives in Chapel Hill, NC with her husband and their furry children. When not writing, she's busy crossing items off her travel bucket list, or chasing eclipses around the globe. She's quirky, consumes way too much coffee, and loves to swim.

ABOUT J.R. THORN

J.R. Thorn is a Reverse Harem Paranormal Romance
Author.

Learn More at:
www.AuthorJRThorn.com

Addicted to Academy? Read more RH Academy by J.R.
Thorn: Fortune Academy, available on Amazon.com!

**Welcome to Fortune Academy, a school where
supernaturals can feel at home—except, I have no
idea what the hell I am.**

Made in the USA
Monee, IL
18 July 2023

38934369R00129